Room 39

&

The Cornish Legacy

By

Mark Simmons

ISBN: 978-1-300-87831-5

PublishNation | London
www.publishnation.co.uk

For Margaret

"So we beat on, boats against the current, borne back

ceaselessly into the past".

F.Scott Fitzgerald: The Great Gatsby. April 1925.

Prologue

September 1982

Now it was over. Waiting for a taxi outside Seaton Barracks Plymouth with its grey accommodation blocks my recent home, the feeling came that life would never be so exciting again, a not altogether unpleasant feeling. Nine years in Her Majesty's Royal Marine Commandos, I had lived with great excitement even terror and great boredom too.

Nine years of life was contained in a pussers suitcase and kit bag. Pussers being Royal Marine slang for any issued kit. It hardly seemed possible.

For me, unlike high ranking officers, no band played me off the base with marshal music. No one to see me off into Civvy Street, just a nod from the main gate guard as if to say 'see you around oppo.' There had been a run-ashore the night before with some of the lads but that had been awkward as if I was already history.

The taxi for North Road station arrived. My kit was confined to the boot, I got in the back. I did not want to pass the time of day with the driver. The taxi pulled out into the traffic flow toward Crown Hill. I did not look back, strange, I felt little other than numbness.

Now it was over, that chapter of my life closed. A new chapter to begin a different challenge, as certain as I could be life would not be lived on the edge again, that's what I thought. How wrong I was.

Part One-Cornwall.

One

Up ahead I saw it as the train bent with the curve of the track. It was bathed in sunshine like an iron gateway to the past. The train slowed on its approach to a crawl. Only a single line crossed the bridge, which bore its simple and fitting inscription on the arch,

'I.K.Brunel
Engineer
1859.'

The Royal Albert Bridge, known by the locals as the Saltash Bridge, just another testament to the genius of its Victorian builder, complete with his 'Brunel truss', two of them four hundred and sixty five foot long and fifty foot above the bridge deck, his trade mark. It was a spectacular crossing over to another world, my past but to the future as well.

A hundred feet and more below languid brown and green lay the expanses of the Tamar River. Natural border between Devon and Cornwall, some would say between Cornwall and England. For crossing that river you cross into a wilder more rugged land. Or that's how it felt to me, more so that day for it was completely unexpected, my return to Cornwall and the past.

The letter that had arrived in my Wimbledon flat two days before had come out of the blue. Addressed to me, Robin Nicolson, with a Cornish postmark, it was a quality envelope, embossed with the title 'Bolitho and Associates Solicitors, Liskeard, Cornwall.'

Perhaps I should have guessed that it would be about Great Aunt Carolyn's recent death, but I did not. No bell rang. The funeral and cremation had been over three weeks ago.

I was not long into my job with Merton Borough Council, as a pen-pusher in the planning department. I had been reluctant to take the time to attend. Not that I had any reason to feel guilty. I did not know Aunt Carolyn that well. My Mother, Aunt, and Cousin had attended the funeral for the family, quite a turn out really.

The will had been 'uncontested' probate going along smoothly, or so my Mother and Aunt thought.

As I slit the envelope open it came to me, 'it must be about good old Aunt Carolyn, she must have left me a little legacy. A few quid would come in handy.' I began to read.

'Dear Mr Robin Nicolson
It is my duty to inform you that you are the sole beneficiary of the late Miss Carolyn Phoebe Thompson's Estate.'

'The sole beneficiary' leapt out, 'my gawd' I thought 'what will Mother say?' One of my sergeant majors' in the Royal Marines used to say 'bite the bullet straight away, it's the best way.' In this case contacting Mother would not be easy, her being 'the bullet.'

It was not long before this I had bought my first property, a pokey flat in Margaret Thatcher's property owning democracy, with a mortgage that stretched away to infinity. The year was 1984. Just over a year before I had left the Royal Marine Commandos, after nine years. Nine years that included the Turkish invasion of Cyprus, a UN tour on the island. Three tours of Northern Ireland on internal security and the Falkland's War. After being shot at by the Greek National Guard, the IRA, and the Argentine Air Force and Army, and only having the pleasure of returning fire and coming to grips with an enemy up close in the Falklands if pleasure was the right emotion, the darkened face of that young Argie was always with me. But let someone else have a go. And physically my yomping days were numbered.

There was no phone in my flat, so I had to wait until I got to work to use the phone. To tell Mother the news, I got to work early.

'Aunt Carolyn has done what?' she said, having near choked on her toast. I repeated the news. It was just after eight, and the office I shared with four others was deserted.

'Why would she do that? You must have been sucking up to her.'

'Don't be daft' I said 'I have not seen her for, what, ten years it must be.'

Mother insisted I call around after work with the offending letter as I knew she would. For there must be some mistake, something I had got wrong was the only answer to her. Men after all could not be trusted with such things.

Two

When I arrived at my parent's house, a 1940's semi built after the Blitz of World War II, my gloom deepened by several notches to see, parked outside, my Aunt's yellow Ford Escort. Aunt Karen, my Mother's younger sister, a right pain in the arse at the best of times. Walking up the path I muttered 'So the inquisition has gathered.'

Knocking on the back door I entered with a cheery 'Hello, anybody home?'

My Mother and Aunt were sat at the table, one of those enamel covered tables; on it were empty tea cups and an open tin of biscuits.

'Here he is' said Mother, as if Aunt Karen did not know who I was. Mother got up and offered me her powdered cheek which I dutifully kissed.

'Let's see it then?' said Aunt Karen as Mother poured me a cup of stewed tea.

'See what?' I acted dumb.

By then my younger sister Joyce and my cousin Lucy and my Father had entered the room from the lounge.

'Give me strength' I thought 'I would rather face a mad Irish mob of rioters with petrol bombs on the Falls Road than this lot.'

The only option was immediate and unconditional surrender. I took the letter from my jacket pocket and to annoy my Aunt, handed it to my Father.

'Oh thanks son' he said surprised. Dad was something of a hen pecked husband, but he sat at the table and with all the authority he could muster read it through aloud for everyone. 'Well there it is, Robin's right', he finished, handing it back toward me, but my Mother clutched it out of mid air, and she and Aunt Karen read it again, as if my Father was bound to have missed something.

'What's 'in contestant' mean?' asked Aunt Karen.

'Recently altered thus delayed' I said confidently, having already looked it up.

'Why should she do that?' said Aunt Karen.

'That's what we'll find out' said Mother, 'I will get right onto it first thing in the morning.'

I was only half listening; more interested in cousin Lucy's short skirt which left little to the imagination. She was stunning and only seventeen. No longer jail-bait I contemplated what our children might be like being first cousins, and then rapidly dismissed the erotic idea remembering that would make Aunt Karen my mother-in-law. By then all four women were chatting away.

'Come and see the garden son' said Dad. He often did this, knowing full well I had little interest in such things, but it gave us space to talk and think. Outside away from the women, we examined his newly planted row of runner beans and the bamboo poles he had arranged wigwam like for them to grow on.

'Here' he said handing me back the letter. He must have picked it up off the table as they were talking and no one had noticed.

'It's addressed to you son. Aunt Carolyn was nobody's fool. She left it to you for a reason. Best thing is, Robin, for you to get down to Cornwall fast and find out why.

Before those two in there', he indicated the house with a jerk of his thumb 'try to take over.'

'Just what I was thinking Dad.'

'Good, Robin.' It was only Mum and Dad who called me Robin to most others I was Rob.

And then we returned to contemplating the climbing qualities of runner beans on bamboo poles.

The next morning from the phone box near my flat, which thankfully had not been vandalised, I rang my office at Merton Borough Council. My boss answered, the type of man who would not be put in charge of a Naafi working party in the corps.

'Leave Rob?' he said 'you cannot have holidays just like that.'

'It's my next-of-kin, I think I can.'

'Oh! Next-of-kin, what have they died?'

'Yes that's right', I did not mention it was weeks ago, or that I was not to my knowledge Aunt Carolyn's next-of-kin.

'OK, five days compassionate leave' and he slammed down the phone.

'Thanks' I said to the dialling tone and hung up.

I did not ring my parents. Best to get down to Cornwall sharpest and sort things out. I took the District line from Wimbledon Broadway to Paddington and within an hour was on the Cornish Riviera express.

Three

On the train I had time to turn over in my mind why my great aunt should leave me her estate. If it had been to stop family friction then it had gone some way to fuel it. Perhaps in some warped way she had done it for that reason. But that was not in her nature from the little I knew of her. Other than that I could come up with nothing. True she had always been affectionate toward me, never missed a birthday, but she was just the same with other members of the family.

It was ten years since I had last seen her, when I had been based with one of the Commando Units in Plymouth, funny it was clear in my mind. My troop had been shooting on the ranges at Tregantle Fort on the Cornish side of the River Tamar. Firing out over the sea, the fort a squat Victorian design that guarded the approaches to Plymouth, one of a ring of forts built during a period of national paranoia about the threat of invasion. Tregantle was only three miles away from Downderry and Aunt Carolyn. So I took a Landrover down there, the troop sergeant was a good egg and did not mind. It was a fine summer's day.

Aunt Carolyn was pleased to see me roll up, especially as I was in uniform, and with the Landrover. Perhaps it would impress the neighbours in her mind. Kantara was just as I remembered it from childhood holidays, a sprawling, airy, large bungalow. Set in a large garden not your typical Cornish bungalow, if there is such a thing in any sense and only a stone's throw from the sea.

Downderry was not your typical Cornish south coast village either. It had been a fishing village once, but with no natural harbour unable to sustain large boats or even many boats come to that. It was all small stuff, mainly crabs and lobsters. By Victorian times it had become a small tourist resort, a bit exclusive as it was not on the main railway line, which it remained down the years, not attracting the summer crowds of nearby Looe or Polperro. But with the coming of motor cars it did grow in the twentieth century, but still remained off the beaten track to a large extent.

For a while I dozed. It did not seem long and the train was arriving at Exeter St.Davids, a station once I had got to know well.

Then the train was moving off. I got a terrible coffee, like sump oil, from the buffet car, more to pass the time than any refreshment value it offered. All too soon we were running beside the Exe River on the southern shore. I wanted to stay awake for that. They came into view clearly on the other shore, the accommodation blocks of the Commando Training centre Lympstone, affectionately referred to as the *'University of Life'* in the Corps of Marines. I wondered at that point how many poor sods were enduring the delights of a mud march in the estuary, or slogging around the assault courses in fighting order with weapons.

Like most people I had been glad to leave the place. Granted I had learnt a lot there but I felt relieved to see it at this remote distance even now. But there had been people I admired. Our recruit troop Colour Sergeant Buster Moore had done everything it was about worth doing. Fought in the Korean War at the Chosen Reservoir, what a campaign that had been. Frozen stiff 'bloody brass monkey weather' he used to call it. Always used to say 'I would never ask you to do anything I would not do myself.' And it was not mere words with him.

If we had a mud march he did it too, not just watched us enduring like some instructors, he must have been about forty-five then, no spring chicken. Even the RSM would defer to him, 'is that alright with you Colour Sergeant Moore?'

'Aye, aye sir just fine' he would say.

The train moved on under a watery sun along the south Devon coast. The line ran between the sea and red cliffs around Teignmouth before turning in land toward Newton Abbot and another stop at its Victorian Station.

Onward south west, skirting to the east of Dartmoor, how many miles had I yomped across that moor I wondered, usually soaking wet and cold. I could still almost feel the soggy dampness, the utter fatigue of it, with ninety pounds of equipment dragging at your back you walked in a kind of half hunched position. Shoulders permanently aching, but it had put me, and countless others, in good stead for the march across the Falklands. There the load carrying was even worse one hundred and twenty pounds plus.

Once ashore at Port San Carlos after a few days watching the Argie Air Force bombing the ships of the task force, we were flown to Mount Kent. Helicopters were in short supply, after the loss of three Chinook's on Atlantic Conveyer when she was sunk thanks to some Argie pilot and a French Exocet missile.

It took two attempts to get to Mount Kent. The company was loaded into Sea Kings and set off right into a 'White-Out' a swirling blanket of thick snow which blots out the pilots reference points. He is blind, there is little in flying more hazardous. Only an instant landing on instruments in which he must have complete trust can avoid disaster. The pilot has to have faith in a few dials and his crewmans mark one eyeballs.

It took us two hours to get back from where we had started on what should have been a half hour flight, the pilots having to land again and again fighting against the blizzard. We were strapped in, in the dark, our hearing drowned by the roaring engines, feeling every shudder of the aircraft as if it might be the last as we ploughed into the ground. The stink of Avcat made us feel sick. But thanks to those matlow pilots we got back in one piece.

A welcome tot of rum greeted us on our return. The CO came round seeing how we felt about trying again the next night. Did we ever have a choice? Some old marine chuckled in the background 'never volunteer for anything.' But there was a determination to get there, to get the job done; this was what we had come to do.

The waiting was not long until dark again; it was dark down there on those islands in winter fourteen hours of the day. Again we climbed aboard those throbbing machines sealed in with the fumes of Avcat about them.

Then we were there. The weather was kind this time. In the hover the helicopter a few feet off the ground, a blast of cold air from the opened door. The klaxon went the exit light turned from red to green and you jumped into the dark. Out and down crawl away in a semicircle of defence for the landing zone. The down draft of the rotor blades drove you down into the ground while the engines deafened you. There was small arms fire away to the north we could see the tracer, and flares lighting the stark landscape as the Sea Kings lifted off and got away. Was it friendly or enemy fire we did not know.

It took us two hours to get up there to the summit of Mount Kent, a couple of bird line miles away, a granite windswept tour. Your boots were soon leaking wet, and there were constant stops as people fell over.

By daylight we were on a tour opposite Mount Kent rising up before us above the cloud and mist. It looked eerie a terrible place. I did not much like the ground in between, no cover and overlooked by the Argies. But there was nothing for it we had to try.

When we got to that narrow valley floor the bloody sun came out. The first time we had seen it in days. On that valley floor was a stone run. Ancient rivers of molten rock that had cooled over millions of years, and broke the ground in wide swathes another natural obstacle for us to cross. Slippery, you could never do it at night with a heavy load; they were bloody awful to cross.

An Argie Pucara ground attack aircraft came sniffing around. If he saw us we were finished. But somehow he did not.

When we got to the summit we found the Argies had legged it in a hurry by the amount of equipment they had left behind. The SBS had hit them as we came in. There was no fighting for us there.

So we huddled among the rocks with the wind and snow constant and gale force it seemed to blow from every direction the temperature well below freezing. We had no green slugs, sleeping bags, no large packs there had been no room in the overloaded choppers, and they could not bring them forward not in that weather. So we munched on cold Argentine rations, and it was me and my oppo to try and stay warm, you found out who your friends were then.

With dawn, bone cold, we could see our next objective across the valley as the mist cleared briefly. Two Sisters and Mount Harriet two separate pinnacles of granite crest lines, barring the road to Stanley.

The weather was seldom clear for any length of time, even a couple of hours of sunshine started drying our sodden clothing when we would steam. But good weather brought the fear of air attack.

So in some ways it was better to be soaked and cold. Each day had its fair share of blizzards and downpours.

Our feet soon began to suffer, 'trench foot' appeared, in feet cold and wet for hours on end.

This was something the First War Tommies suffered from not us, but we did. When the green slugs and large packs finally arrived you might get them dry for an hour or two with clean socks. But it was soon back to wet boots and socks you hoarded your dry socks. Wet footwear produced blisters. The next thing would be frost bite. With the wind chill it was down to minus 30 centigrade sometimes.

And then there was Mount Harriet my appointment with destiny. 'Fix bayonets' came the order, whenever had we been ordered to do that other than in training to stick it in a straw dummy. Through the minefields at night where every step could be your last, a half mile to the objective. I remembered hoping the Argies would have legged it.

But no they were there. We saw them as spectres among the crags and rocks. We sent in 66mm and 84mm anti-tank rockets and charged yelling screaming like furies. Argentines were throwing down their arms and raising hands in surrender some uttered the word 'comrade.' But others tried to resist.

One loomed up in front of me tried to turn his rifle on me. I never hesitated, drove my bayonet into his neck felt it snap against something hard I fired at the same time no squeezing the trigger just a sharp jerk. The 7.62 bullet flung him back against a boulder. I let him have another round just to make sure as he slid to the ground. 'You'll have to be quicker than that mate' I yelled and spat on him as I passed. Why did I have to do that?

It was not all one sided. One Corporal was killed, another hit in both legs taking out a heavy machine gun. Two horribly injured by mines. And others fell on that bloody hill.

It was nearly light by the time the position was finally cleared, Strewn amongst the rocks were all manner of weapons and equipment and unmoving grey clad figures. Checked out for any sign of life then marked as dead by an upturned rifle supporting a helmet. They had once been living breathing men.

Soon after that, thankfully, it was all over, the surrender. A stranger who had seen us then might have wondered who had won. Dark spectres of men we were walking jerkily on sodden sore feet like robots. Filthy all over red eyes staring out of blackened faces. But no the stranger would see too a grim gritty determination.

The funny thing was about the bayonet that I snapped against the Argie, which must have struck his spine through the neck. I got charged for damaging kit had to pay for a replacement twenty-seven pounds thank you Marine Nicolson 'that will teach you to look after your kit' said the armourer sergeant back in barracks who had never gone to the Falklands. Bloody hell it cost me twenty-seven pounds to kill the Queen's enemies. Still got that broken bayonet, a weird memento.

But some had paid a much higher price. Somewhere in one of those Dartmoor moorland churchyards we were passing lay the body of an oppo killed on those windswept, bloody freezing islands.

There was a young woman sat opposite me reading a newspaper, I could see the headlines on the front page. *'Talks between the Miners and the National Coal Board broke down.'* It seemed the country was fighting a civil war. Had we really fought that war two thousand miles away so that riot police could battle miners on the streets? What a country I thought.

I returned to gazing out the window. We would soon be in Plymouth, Guz as it was known affectionately in the services. How many runs ashore had I been on there but there would be no time this trip to sample the delights of Union Street.

All too soon it was North Road Station Plymouth, and then across the Royal Albert Bridge and into Cornwall. Past Wearde Quay Saltash at the entrance of the Lynher River where it joined the Tamar across Antony Passage out into open Cornish country. That rugged land, here the gorse lining the railway embankments seemed higher, the yellow flowers more intense, brighter.

Then crossing over the Lynher again, higher this time, on the St Germans viaduct another marvel of railway engineering, briefly stopping at the small village of St Germans with its tiny railway station. On through open countryside small fields divided by Cornish dry stone hedges, until finally the train reached my destination the town of Liskeard.

Four

Holdall in hand I got off the train at Liskeard some twenty miles from Plymouth. I walked along Station Road into the small market town, where I got bed and breakfast at the friendly if, seedy, Fountain Hotel for the night. The landlady told me where the offices of Bolitho and Associates' were. Most of the evening I passed in the bar with the locals, there was much talk about the situation *'up north'* with unanimous support for the miners *'salt of the earth'* tempered with *'the unions need sorting out.'* An odd stance but one many including me, I suppose, took.

At nine the next morning, a grey overcast day threatening rain, I presented myself at Bolitho and Associates'. A middle aged female secretary behind large glasses, told me that Mr Manton, who was dealing with the case, would see me shortly, and offered me tea or coffee which I declined, having just filled up on the Fountain Hotel's *'full English breakfast.'* So I was ushered into the well healed waiting room. The furniture, if old, was quality and well polished. On a coffee table were current copies of *'Cornish Life'* and *'Horse and Hound.'* So it looked like the practice was doing well.

'Mr Nicolson, I'm Anthony Manton' said a short but powerfully built man, entering the room after five minutes, extending his hand. His shake was firm; he looked about my age early thirties. He had a thick neck, encircled by collar and tie, in which, he looked decidedly uncomfortable. He would be more at home in a gym, in a tracksuit, rather than here. I put him down as a rugby player prop forward with that build.

He led me to his office exchanging pleasantries about my journey to Cornwall and where I had stayed.

Manton's office like the waiting room was well appointed and tidy. So they ran a tight ship I thought. On his large desk was a thin file, I read it upside down. *'Miss Carolyn Phoebe Thompson.'*

'So you're not a Bolitho, Mr Manton, but an associate' I said sitting down opposite him.

'In fact Mr Nicolson, there is only one Bolitho left at the firm, Mr Richard, and he just comes in part time now. He will be eighty shortly.'

Manton opened the file and read through it. 'All straight forward Mr Nicolson, basically your Aunt left everything to you. Now can you prove your identity?'

My driving licence, passport, and Bolitho and associates' own letter to me covered that request.

'I wonder if you can tell me Mr Manton, did my Aunt change her will recently.'

He looked down at the file. 'Yes she did about a year ago. She left you a letter.' He slid it across the desk to me.

'Read it later' I said putting it in my holdall.

'As you wish Mr Nicolson, no doubt your Aunt will explain all in the letter. Here are the keys to Kantara the bungalow at Downderry. Probate should be completed as quickly as possible, it may be a few months but we will send you a cheque for the contents of bank accounts etc, less our fees' he smiled.

'Your Aunt used to employ a gardener handyman. Let's see' he glanced at the file 'a Mr Longman, William I think, bit of an odd cove. But we kept him on a few hours a week to look after the place. We have tried to get in touch with him, but he seems to have disappeared over the last few days. No doubt he will get in touch when he sees you about and introduce himself. Was hoping he would be there today, no matter I will run you over to Downderry. I take it you intend staying there?'

'Yes I do, I expect there will be odds and ends to sort out. No problem with probate?' I asked.

'No it's fine to stay there.'

Manton took me out to the car park and we climbed into his new model Rover. I was a little surprised Manton was taking me to Kantara. I supposed it was all part of the service, and no doubt would show up in the fees.

'Kantara, that's an unusual name?' said Manton, starting the engine.

'It comes from Cyprus a crusader castle up in the Kyrenian Mountains, there is a hill station nearby of the same name. My Aunt spent many years on Cyprus and quite a bit of the time at that station where her father had a bungalow.'

'Of course' he said 'there is a property in the will on Cyprus you have inherited, deeds and all we will send on to you after probate. Mind you I don't know how you will fair taking possession of it with the situation in Northern Cyprus.'

'Have you been my Aunt Carolyn's solicitor long Mr Manton?'

'No not long' he said as we left the car park 'it was young Mr Bolitho up to a few months ago, bit misleading he was not young, he was just the younger brother.'

'What happened to Bolitho then, retired?' I asked just to make conversation really.

'No, sadly not. It was John Bolitho; he was coming up for retirement, had even cut his hours down. Got killed in a traffic accident a few months back.'

'Oh I'm sorry' I said. 'Just trying to get a bit of background on my Aunt Carolyn, bit odd we have found it. My family that is, that she should leave everything to me.'

'I see' said Manton.

Which meant really he did not, it was a pity about John Bolitho, being 'killed in a traffic accident' for sure he would have known my Aunt, better than Manton did after only a few months. Yet how well did solicitors really know their clients. But I sat back, forgetting that, and enjoyed the drive from Liskeard out toward the south coast along the Looe road. The hedgerows were full of spring flowers. At Nomansland we turned off the Looe road.

At Hessenford, another hamlet of a few cottages and a pub, Manton took the road sign posted Seaton and Downderry. A narrow road wound its way through a small steep sided valley, thick with trees. Finally emerging from the wood around a bend the broad expanses of the sea was to our front, beyond a grey sandy beach. Lining the edge of the road on the beach side were concrete sentinels' like a row of teeth with big gaps. Put there in the Second World War to thwart German invaders trying to get tanks ashore. On the inland side of the road were lined rows of holiday caravans, this was Seaton, named after the river which emerged here no more than a stream running into the sea. The place was deserted, too early yet for the summer visitors.

Manton continued east along the coast road, within a mile we were in the village of Downderry, bigger than Seaton. With Victorian terraced houses, old fisherman's cottages, and modern bungalows clustered around a small central square.

Just past the centre Manton turned right toward the sea, grey like the day, and then left into a small street marked *'Private.'*

Here were older bungalows and at the end of this cul-de-sac on the left in its own large garden stood Kantara.

It was an odd bungalow for this part of the world. Even odd compared to the other seven bungalows that shared the cul-de-sac, Kantara had a lot of wood, more like a house you might come across in the Southern United States, or some alpine lodge. A veranda ran five feet wide all round the bungalow supported by pillars between ground and roof. There was a detached garage and store. Most of the garden was lawn with shrubs, palm trees, and Monterey pines for shade.

Kantara, had been built to my Aunt's design and owed more to the military prefabricated wooden bungalows used throughout the British Empire by the Colonial Service. One of which my Aunt had lived in while on Cyprus at the remote hilltop station of Kantara at the eastern end of the Kyrenian Mountain range stretching toward the Karpass Peninsula, where my Aunt's family had retreated to trying to escape the baking summer heat of Nicosia. Obviously she had tried to create that same bungalow here in Cornwall.

I explained all this to Manton. 'I did think it a little out of place. You have the keys Mr Nicolson, would you like me to come in with you.'

'No it's alright' I said, we shook hands and I got out of the car, and picked up my holdall from the back seat, Manton turned the Rover in Kantara's drive and he was gone.

Five

Taking the keys from my pocket, for a few moments I just stood there staring at Kantara. Glancing up the street at the other bungalows, all was deserted nothing moved no curtain twitched no neighbour making an approach.

With what I felt was a decisive spring in my step I walked down the path, and up the three steps onto the veranda and to the front door. The Yale key easily opened the door onto a long corridor which ran the length of the bungalow to the kitchen at the back, if my memory was right. Doors were on both sides of the corridor for lounges and bedrooms. It smelt musty and damp, which was not surprising as it had been empty for months.

Dumping my holdall on the large corridor table, I picked up the telephone; it had a clear dialling tone. Manton had said he would get it re-connected when I phoned from Wimbledon, well that was quick I thought given BT were not renowned for working that fast. But this was Cornwall I decided things were different down here. Mind you, another thought struck me, once Mother twigged it she would be on my back every day.

Entering every room I opened the windows to get some air circulating. In the kitchen there was no food or makings, unusual but then, perhaps Bolitho and Associates had cleared that out using the handyman, the odd elusive Mr Longman.

The lounge was untidy, book shelves and desk with stuff shoved in all sorts of positions. I looked through the books in the large bookcase. Aunt Carolyn certainly had a lot, must be hundreds of them, and a lot on World War II. Strange, it struck me, for a maiden aunt. And there was a copy of *'From Russia with Love'* never read her as a thriller reader. I slid it off from the bookshelf. A hardback copy, with its distinctive Richard Chopping cover, of a red rose steam going through the trigger of a pistol; it was a 1957 first edition.

But what grabbed my attention was the inscription on the title page, it read...

'To Carolyn affectionately. We stopped him finding the big secret Ian Fleming.'

Well you are a dark horse Carolyn I thought, fancy my Aunt knowing Ian Fleming. But then I seemed to remember she had been in publishing for a while. Further along the shelf I came across another Bond book, another first edition of *'You Only Live Twice'* 1964, another Chopping cover with a toad his right forward leg trapping a dragon fly under it, above the toad a pink chrysanthemum I had a vague memory of reading this one, set in Japan as I recalled. Inside it was inscribed.

'To Carolyn affectionately Ian Fleming.'

I looked for others but could not find any.

Sitting at the open roll top desk, I aimlessly pulled things out, there was so much there I could not close it. I did not relish having to go through that lot. Nothing seemed to ring a bell. Then I remembered the letter retrieving it from my holdall on the hall table. Back at the desk I opened it with my Aunt's letter opener in the shape of a miniature sword. It looked like it had a miniature White Ensign on the hilt which had been near rubbed away with use. It began.

'Dear Robin

I expect this is something of a shock to you. However it will be worse for me because if you are reading this I will be dead, and not of natural causes, but murdered.

I cannot tell you why or who you will have to work that out for yourself. The mere fact you have this letter should rule out Bolitho and Associates who I have been with for years. But a word of warning you must trust no one young man, if you value your life.

I think you will have the open mind I am looking for. And as a former Commando the determination I hope to see it through. Did any of you ever wonder why I came to Cornwall? This quest has consumed over half my life. But I have been getting pretty close.

I hope you will find Kantara as much a home as I have; I give it to you. And my quest too as a sacred trust.

All my love and hopes.

Aunt Carolyn.'

'So' I said out loud. 'Aunt Carolyn an easy task for once'. Were these the ravings of an old woman? Although she had never struck me as having lost her marbles, on the other hand I had not seen her for, what, six or seven years, and before that only perhaps ten times in twenty.

Putting the letter back in its envelope, I got up and slowly went from room to room. What I was looking for I had no idea.

With nothing in the bungalow, in the form of food and drink I gave up my fruitless search and went in search of provisions. Locking Kantara, I kept the letter on me and walked slowly into the heart of Downderry which took little more than five minutes, finding the village hall and post office and Spar shop. Inside the shop I passed the time of day with the woman behind the counter.

'You'm Miss Thompson's nephew then, she was well liked in this village, real lady, not like some I could mention.'

'I'm sorry to say I did not see her in the last years of her life. I was abroad in the service.'

'You'm the Marine, she talked about you especially in the Falklands War. She was as bright as a button to the end. Getting a bit frail, but lovely way to go, heart attack weren't it?'

'So I believe.'

'Staying long?'

'Oh a few days, things to sort out.'

'Now her doctor was the Canadian woman, nice she is. I recall your Aunt saying how much she liked her.'

'Ere Stan' she shouted to a fat man stacking shelves. 'What's that new doctor called the Canadian one?'

'Reilly' he shouted back without turning 'Doctor Eve Reilly, can't you remember anything woman and she's not new been here eighteen months now.'

'There you are, Eve Reilly, don't take no notice of him, and you be?'

I told her.

'Rob Nicolson' she repeated 'now if you wants' to see Doctor Reilly about your Aunt make an appointment, surgery's just across the road there. She will give you all the gen on your Aunt's health and all.'

'Do you know where I might find William Longman; I believe he did odd jobs and gardening for my Aunt?'

'How long you been here Mr Nicolson?'

'A couple of hours just arrived.'

'Don't you fret then Bill Longman he'll find you.'

With that I paid for my groceries and left. Calling at the surgery a formidable looking receptionist sat behind a large desk, thin and waspish looking she eyed me with suspicion.

'You're not one of Doctor Reilly's patients' she answered my enquiry to see the Doctor.

'No I'm not, you're right there' I smiled trying to lighten the atmosphere with little success. 'I would like to see her on a personal matter' I hurried on under the scrutiny. 'She was my late Aunt's Doctor, Miss Thompson.'

'She is extremely busy, I'll see what I can do' she said dismissively.

'That's alright I'm staying at Kantara' she looked up as if to say *'you still here'* and nodded.

Weighed down with carrier bags I walked back to Kantara. At the end of the road leading to Kantara a brown Ford Cortina was parked, one man sat in it reading the 'The Sun' newspaper odd I thought parked there. If this had been Northern Ireland it would have required a *'Sit Rep.'* But this was Cornwall and I was not on patrol, and people did not blow each other up, he was merely waiting for someone, I moved on.

In Kantara I made myself an instant coffee and returned to the lounge and my Aunt's letter; I reread it three times. It was odd she hoped I would *'find Kantara a home'* surely she knew I was unlikely to keep it. I got up and walked around the large lounge examining things at random. The walls were full of pictures. Three of Cornish landscapes, a photo of what looked like a World War II submarine entering harbour, I guessed by the look of it Port Said or Alexandria, four men could be clearly seen in the conning tower. Pictures of two smiling young women one was a Wren, they had their arms around each other, and the one in civilian dress was Aunt Carolyn, the other, the wren, my Grandmother Elizabeth. It looked like the backdrop was Trafalgar Square.

Next was an oil painting of a castle high up looking out toward the distant sea from its ruined battlements. It had an armature feel to it, in the corner it was signed Carolyn Thompson Kantara Castle 1939.

'Surely not' I thought taking it down from the wall. It was two feet square in a good frame. Turning it around to look at the back I felt something move inside. With that there came a loud knock at the door.

Six

 Framed in the open door was a giant of a man who blocked out some of the light. He was dressed in worn blue overalls with sandals on his large bare feet. A huge unkempt bushy ginger beard covered his chin, his hair was long. From this mass of hair his blue eyes examined me intensely.

'William Longman I presume' I said extending my hand and introducing myself thinking what an apt name he had. My hand disappeared in his shovel like hand surprisingly his grip was not a bone crusher.

'Call me Bill' he said, in a deep voice.

'Come in' I beckoned him.

He shrugged his shoulders and walked in stooping to avoid the door lintel, I led him to the kitchen.

'Coffee or tea?' I asked.

'Tea' he said.

'Did you know my Aunt long, Bill?'

'Yep, years, good woman she was.'

He was obviously a man of few words. I poured the tea and handed him the mug, into which he ladled four heaped spoons of sugar.

'Bill, I was quite surprised, well the whole family was that I was left Kantara.' He made no comment so I went on. 'She left me a letter' again no comment. So I told him about the contents.

Bill nodded when I finished. For a moment I thought he would make no comment to that. He slurped his tea noisily.

'Your Aunt was on to some'it big. She came across it in the war. It had to do with the Allan-Cleary's, big noise landowners around here, got a big old house up Maker way.' He indicated toward the east with his tea mug. 'If you're Aunt was murdered and I 'spect she was it ad some'it to do with they.' He put his mug down. 'Few weeks ago she said she was getting close.'

'Close to what?' I asked.

Bill shrugged his shoulders. 'Don't really know other than it had something to do with the Government, and I don't trust they fellers remember them from the war. Think she was about to spill the beans to the press. Do you want me to carry on with the garden?'

'Yes, yes please' I said, his last question and change of direction had thrown me.

'Cash in hand Mr Nicolson.'

'Yes of course.'

With that he ambled out the back door toward the garden shed. His comment about the Government had thrown me a bit. And who were the Allan-Cleary's. He had to know more than that but I was a stranger to him. With that I returned to the lounge and the picture of Kantara I had left on the sofa. With a knife it was easy to move the backing paper away from the frame. Inside were three soft back lined exercise books, the type I had used at school years ago. They were marked on the covers *'Journal of Carolyn Thompson'* and numbered one, two, and three. I started with one.

It was dated January 1942. I began to read my Aunt's clear handwriting.

'January 1942, Nicosia, Cyprus.

I, that is Carolyn Thompson, begin this journal to try and find the truth, from all the rumours and what my Father told me. And for the sake of Joe wherever he is and the baby, his baby, our baby, another victim of this, I lost. I hope Joe is a prisoner but I doubt it, in my heart I know he is gone. Joe is Joseph Lock a sergeant in the Commandos.

That's the place to start and I must stick to the point. The Commandos came to Cyprus in April 1941. It was a bad time for us the British and the war. We were kicked out of Greece and Crete the Germans seemed unbeatable. There was a revolution in Iraq trouble in Syria with the Vichy French.

27

My Father, James Thompson, was a District Commissioner for the Empire Office on Cyprus. We have been here over ten years. He worked closely with the Governor, being a senior Commissioner. With the coming of the war he worked with various military officers as they came and went. There was a bit of a flap the Germans might invade Cyprus like Crete with their paratroops but they did not.

He felt there was more to Britain's military woes in the Mediterranean than just German Military brilliance that some third clandestine effort was at hand. Cyprus, throughout its history was a crossroads. As it was then perhaps a backwater but crossroads all the same. It is only forty miles from the Turkish coast; the island had a large Turkish population. Turkey was neutral true but its sympathies lay with Germany.

From Ankara the Germans had their best window on the world; their embassy had a big Reich Security Department. People were often not what they seemed.

But I must go back. It was a weekend in May 1941 I met Sergeant Joseph Lock. Dear Joe, he was so handsome and full of life. But I don't think I fell for him that quickly. It may appear so now. But I suppose the war heightened awareness; you never knew what might happen. Although a Royal Artillery soldier Joe was a commando. He had volunteered for them as soon as he could, did all the training in Scotland, his homeland. Although to hear him speak you would hardly have thought him a Scotsman. Even then at the start of the Commandos I knew they had a dangerous job.

Joe had been lucky on Crete 600 of the 800 men who went there with Layforce, named after Colonel Robert Laycock their CO, were killed or captured. They came back under a cloud, it was said that the officers had saved their own skins, instead of covering the retreat.

Father entertained some of them, called it 'doing his bit', had them stay at Kantara, we had a bungalow there at the eastern end of the Kyrenian Mountains, they came in small groups for R&R. I helped entertain them; swimming expeditions and walking by day, cocktail parties at night, the war seemed a long way off.

So that's how I met Joe, a lowland Scot, such a gentle man softly spoken bit of a plum in his voice really. Tall a bit skinny, thin legs in his shorts, but handsome, the last man you might think of as a commando. We became lovers, we planned to marry, and perhaps we should have before he went on that last op. But we did not; it seemed to be tempting fate.

Father used to confide in me at the time. Mum had died ten years before, and my elder sister by five years Elizabeth, 'Lizzy', was in the UK in the Wrens. The trouble was then, my head was full of Joe and I did not take much notice of my Father. Or the awkward looking, RNVR naval officer, Lieutenant Commander Mike Foote, my Father seemed to spend so much time with.

Mike arrived on Cyprus in June 1941. Father told me in confidence he was in Naval Intelligence, and had come to find the Ankara web on the island, if there was one. Mike worked under Commander Allan-Cleary the naval attaché.'

There was that name again, Allan-Cleary, for the second time in an hour. What was it Bill had said? *'Big noise landowners'* and *'If you're Aunt was murdered it ad some'it to do with they.'* Which Allan-Cleary I wondered, and read on with heightened interest.

'Joe and his unit left their canvas camp near the ancient site of Salamis in August for Egypt. A few weeks later I knew I was pregnant.

My father was always an understanding man. I told him straight away and who the father was. Secretly I think he was pleased, and promised to try and find out where Joe was. That commitment to me and interest in Joe, I now realise, was to cost my father his life. I wrote to Joe, whether he ever got the letter I don't know.

It was Mike Foote, who got the 'buzz' on 'The Raid on Rommel'. He found the message from MI6 in London that Rommel was not even in Libya but in Rome, with his wife Lucie, before the raid took place.

Allan-Cleary had got it before Mike, he was then at GHQ in Cairo but sat on it. Rommel had been in Rome since 1st November, Ultra at Bletchley Park had decoded a message from German Army Enigma. They could have called off 'Operation Flipper' saved the commandos that died and with them my dear, Joseph. But they did not, was it merely an administration cock-up or something else. And it alerted Allan-Cleary to Ultra but it was just a word to him then.

Mike Foote dug into it. Why had they risked valuable submarines? Allan-Cleary told him on his return to Cyprus the lid was kept on it for fear of compromising Auchinleck's proposed invasion of Libya, 'Operation Crusader', due to kick-off on 18th November. Mike thought that rubbish, a smoke screen, and it convinced him something was wrong with Allan-Cleary. He began to dig Richard (Dick) Peter Allan-Cleary, then Commander RNVR; home was a manor house, Gweebarra, at Maker Heights just across Plymouth sound on the Cornish side. The family home for centuries was in the Republic of Ireland, an estate in Donegal.

Dick Allan-Cleary had been a weekend sailor with the RNVR, sometime before the outbreak of war. Mike never quite nailed how Dick had got into naval intelligence. He hinted at the old-boy network and the murky London Clubs, thus he had become a field operator, an attaché, moving in the highest circles of Britain's High Command. But he was careful, never giving much away, he was cold and calculating. But that was not enough to make him a double agent, a spy, in fact really his manner was well suited for the job he did.

It was at Government House in Nicosia I met him for the first time, around Christmas 1941, it was a Christmas party. Dad made me go insisting it would lift my spirits after the loss of Joe. I don't think he was looking for a husband for me or anything like that. He would never do that, not my father.

Mike Foote was there. It was a Friday 19 December, the whole island, if not the whole world was agog about the Japanese attack on Pearl Harbour and Germany and Italy declaring war on the Americans.

I suppose, I was still depressed and probably looked a sight. Mike introduced me to Allan-Cleary, he danced with me once. He had little to say, and neither did I.

Later Mike asked me what I thought of Allan-Cleary. Thought, I thought nothing at the time. All I could get out of Mike was that there was something 'odd' about him, something 'not quite right'.

Eventually Mike told my Father of his suspicions'. At first my Father did not believe it. He said Mike had a 'fertile imagination and these intelligence fellows were all the same.'

Yet he did supply other, I suppose you would call it, circumstantial evidence. Cyprus could easily have been taken by the Germans in the early summer of 1941. There were only a handful of defenders then until part of an Australian division arrived, although they spent much of their time getting blind drunk on the local wine in Famagusta.

Then there was a deception plan dummy guns, airfields, bunkers, aircraft, real 'works of art' Mike called them. There was a dummy airfield near Paphos. All betrayed to Italian Intelligence, how?

As 1942 came, Mike or my Father, must have made a mistake, for somehow they alerted Allan-Cleary he was suspected, for he murdered them, I have no doubt whatsoever about that now.

Mike and Dad went up into the Troodos Mountains one day. It was early January 1942; I was suffering with morning sickness. They went to visit the wounded, which came here from the desert war to convalesce at the Forest Park Hotel at Platres. The hotel was being used as a military hospital then, being cool in the summer months in the mountains and bracing in winter. They were coming back, at night; their car ran off the road. My Father was driving; he was a good driver and knew that mountain road well. There was snow on the ground and it was icy. Dad was killed instantly.

Mike was severely injured and not discovered until the next day, by then he was suffering from exposure as well, he was taken back to the Forest Park Hospital.

Kemal Faiz, a Turkish Cypriot Superintendent of Police always polite and immaculate in his turn out, came to see me and broke the news as gently as he could. What a job poor man. I insisted he take me to see Mike there and then. He refused, not at that time of the day but agreed reluctantly he would do so the next day. At that time of the year we stayed at the flat in Nicosia, the bungalow at Kantara was closed up for the short winter.

The next day Kemal Faiz picked me up and we drove up into the Troodos Mountains. He put a blanket around me. He was very concerned to be taking a pregnant woman who had had a recent shock on such a trip. It was a long run in those days; it took most of the day there and back from Nicosia. Snow was still on the ground around the high Troodos.

Close to Platres, Kemal parked the car near a bend, and went off, saying he would not be long. I thought it was a call of nature. As we set off again and rounded a bend, I saw, down in a steep ravine, my Father's car.

'Is this the place Superintendent?'

He nodded. 'Yes Miss, the Sergeant at Platres asked me to take a look at it.'

'Why would he do that?'

'For the report details.'

I felt he was holding something back. Trying to save me further hurt.

'My Father was a good driver Superintendent, he knew this road well.'

'Yes Miss, but the ice and the snow at night would be extremely tricky. It might catch out the best driver we must keep an open mind.'

With that the phone rang. I put down the journal, and went out into the hall to answer it.

'Hello.'

'Mr Nicolson, Doctor Reilly here' said a clear North American female voice.

'Ah Doctor thank you for calling I wonder if I could see you about my Aunt the late Miss Thompson.'

'Yes certainly, anything to help, could you call at the surgery, say three this afternoon?'

I readily agreed, and returned to the lounge and Cyprus and the snow covered Troodos Mountains.

'At the Forest Park we were allowed to see Mike, his head was bandaged he had a fractured skull, broken leg and arm. The young army doctor was not hopeful.

Kemal and the Doctor left the room to talk leaving me alone with Mike. I sat beside his bed in the private room.

Suddenly his eyes opened and he looked directly at me. He mumbled something I did not understand. I got up to call the Doctor. Then I heard distinctly.

'Run off the road. He's White Fang.' That was all. Then he closed his eyes. By the time I had fetched the Doctor, Mike had relapsed into the coma. I told the Doctor Mike had been garbled.

However on the return to Nicosia I told Kemal Faiz, what he had said. 'That's why you stopped to look at the car Superintendent isn't it, there's something wrong with it?'

He nodded. 'There is on the right hand side damage and paint from another vehicle, camouflage paint it looks like from a military vehicle'.

'There must be hundreds of those on the island.'

'Yes, and of course it is still more than likely to have been an accident. Miss Thompson, have you any idea what the reference to 'White Fang' might mean, other than the Jack London novel?'

Kemal did not mention that small word 'He's' I had a good idea, but what did White Fang mean? Who or what was White Fang?

'And of course' the Superintendent continued 'your Father's car may have been in an accident previously which had not been repaired, I will have to check with the transport pool.'

'To investigate Superintendent' I said.

'Indeed Miss.'

I don't know why, for I did not know him well, but I had confidence in Superintendent Kemal Faiz of the Cyprus Police, the man oozed confidence, this man would leave no stone unturned. But Mike had said clearly 'Run off the road.' Provided he recovered all would be revealed.'

'Mr Nicolson, you there?' echoed Bill's voice from the kitchen.

"Up here Bill" I called.

He ambled into the lounge. 'I'm leaving now be back soon.'

'Right, good Bill.'

He looked around the room. 'Gawd you been lookin for some'it, it's like a tip?'

'This is how I found it Bill.'

'You don't say, well your Aunt was a tidy person, everything in its place.

If it's not you then someone has been looking for some'it.' With that he ambled away.

So someone had been here looking for what? What I held in my hand, how would they know, and who were they? I scratched my head. This was ridiculous.

It was nearing lunch. I had noticed the Inn-on-the-Shore watering hole during my walk around the village. A bite there and a drink before seeing Doctor Reilly would be good. The journals were not that big, I would take them with me. With that I returned the picture of Kantara to its place on the wall.

Seven

The Inn-on-the-Shore was quiet at lunch time. A few well chosen questions to the landlady got me no further. My Aunt was not a regular there. Which did not surprise me. So I changed tack, after ordering the fish pie and a pint of the local bitter.

'Do you know the Allan-Cleary's at all?'

'Of course' waiting for the froth to settle on my beer, 'well not know as it is,' she said placing the beer on the bar, the landlady was middle aged with middle aged spread and an ample cleveage. 'I know of them. As most people round these parts. Big landowners, used to be quite a naval family. But the son, Martin, did not follow the tradition that way. The old man must be getting on now. People say he never got to admiral as if he should have, do you know what I mean?'

I nodded then asked 'What's the son do then?'

'Oh, fingers in all sorts of pies. Property, got a pub or two, not this one though, and a small boat building firm owns land around here. They got an estate in Ireland too.'

With that she was drawn away to serve another customer. Taking my beer I headed toward a table by a window that overlooked the beach. On the walls were some old framed photos of Downderry and the coast. A row of radar aerials and a generator building caught my eye. *'Part of the early warning defence radar 1940,'* read the caption. Others were Victorian with overdressed people on the beach. At the table I took out the journals and started reading again.

'Sadly Mike did not regain consciousness and died two days after my visit to the Forest Park hospital.

We buried Father at the Protestant Cemetery in Kyrenia. It was a wet day a few people from Government House turned out, but not the Governor or Allan-Cleary. Mike was buried at the military cemetery in Nicosia. The duty officer was there, a young Army Lieutenant; he told me Allan-Cleary had left the island, to where he was not sure. Hours after Mike's funeral I had a miscarriage, so I lost the baby as well. I had lost everything, how pitiful I was. I spent several days in hospital.

It must have been a month later before I saw Superintendent Kemal Faiz again, by which time I had recovered physically. I had to search him out. But he was genuinely pleased to see me.

In his office alone I asked him about the investigation. He told me he had started checking the military bases and the movement of vehicles. However within days of doing so he was summoned to Government House where he was told he was off the case. It was soon closed with the verdict accidental death. He was distressed to learn I had not been told.

'Taken off the case by who?' I asked.

'I do not know Miss Thompson.'

His eyes looked blank, but the Turks always had that air of inscrutability about them, and I could not read Kemal Faiz. Then a brief smile crossed his face.

'Between us Miss, as I left Government house in my car on that day, I passed a parked Humber staff car in olive drab paint with a crumpled wing. I took the number and finally treading carefully, found out it was out on the day of your Father's accident. It had been booked out to staff at Government House. From the panel beater who repaired it I found out it had hit another vehicle, a black vehicle.'

'My father's Ford was black.'

Kemal Faiz nodded. 'Indeed there are many black vehicles, all this is circumstantial evidence. And they left it late repairing the Humber if indeed it was the car. But, he opened his hands to make the point 'to be taken off the case, at first glance a motor accident, well you must judge for yourself. But I find it odd and I am not pleased. Never pleased to leave a case in such circumstances. But sometimes we are mere pawns in the great scheme of things.'

My meal arrived and I put the journal away. I took a drink of beer and began to eat, thinking all the time. Turning it over.

Most of it, I had to agree with the good Superintendent Kemal Faiz, so far anyway, was circumstantial, but there was a lot of it. And then there was Lieutenant Mike's deathbed evidence, which was powerful. Although only my Aunt had heard it and she must have been pretty upset at the time, could she have imagined it? No, I dismissed that quickly, why would she. The Lieutenant and Carolyn's father had been convinced there was something wrong with Allan-Cleary. The car taken from the Government House motor pool, where Allan-Cleary worked sometimes and then there was 'White Fang' I had heard that before but where?

My lunch was good for pub-grub, and plenty of it. I washed it down with another pint, and then thought better of having another as I would see Doctor Reilly soon. So instead I took a walk along the beach.

The radar aerials were long gone now but I did come across one of the concrete bases the pylons had been bolted to. Crumbling now but obvious what they were.

Walking toward Seaton I regained the road and walked along it back to Downderry. The weather was trying to improve it was definitely brighter.

At the surgery I only had to wait a few minutes for my appointment, under the gaze of the same waspish receptionist.

There came a buzz on some sort of intercom. 'Doctor Reilly's ready for you' said the wasp, pointing toward a corridor.

Doctor Eve Reilly was younger than I had expected in her late twenties I guessed. We shook hands across her desk. Her shake was strong for a woman, her grip firm.

'Mr Nicolson, good to see you, anything I can do to help, fire away.'

Her accent was not as pronounced off the phone. She had short, blonde hair making her face rounded. The blue grey eyes examined me thoroughly. She wore tight fitting jeans and a light V necked jumper over her slim figure.

'What do you think of that Doctor?' I asked handing her my Aunt's letter.

She read it through slowly, probably more than once, the blue grey eyes running from line to line, her lips moving slightly with the words.

'I see' she said handing back the letter. 'Now you want me to say whether this is the ravings of a deranged elderly woman, or?' she left that hanging in the air.

'Exactly Doctor.'

'Call me Eve' she said 'most people do, Doctor Eve if you like.'

'O.K Eve, so what do you think?'

'I did not see your aunt, Carolyn Thompson much Mr Nicolson. I checked before you came in, three times in the eighteen months I have been here. However on the last occasion in the surgery I found her blood pressure rather high. She had a cold too. We got her to lie down quietly for a while, in the nurses' room. Her blood pressure came down quite a bit so I let her go home, not that we could make her stay. She seemed quite sensible to me.

But I was worried. I rang her the next morning saying I would call on her after surgery, about this time it would have been, to check her blood pressure again and if necessary prescribe some medication. I did not think hospitalisation would be necessary.

When I got there she did not answer my knock, the door was unlocked. I found her dead in the corridor. I tried to revive her, but it was no good, she had by then probably been dead for two or three hours. Heart attack certainly. One of the reasons I agreed to see you Mr Nicolson, is I blame myself to a certain extent. But your Aunt was elderly, had a cold, and who knows when anybody might have a heart attack. You see Mr Nicolson; medical science is not an exact science. Partly I expected you to accuse me of negligence, or something, but I did think your Aunt was quite strong for her age. And now you have put another different dimension on it.'

She put her hands together as if praying, resting her thumbs on her lips obviously thinking. Her skin I noticed was almost flawless.

'Was she bonkers Eve?' I asked.

She smiled broadly at that. 'Who is sane Mr Nicolson?'

'Call me Rob, Eve.'

'One observation I would make if she was suffering some form of mental illness, I saw no evidence of it, not that I was looking for it. So, perhaps, we must presume there is truth in the letter as far as she was concerned Rob.'

'Mm' I said thinking 'one thing is true about it, the letter that is, she did end up dead.'

'Yes true, pity she did not date the letter?'

'No, but on the other hand it was within the last few months she changed her will.'

'One thing Rob, you have not taken her good advice about trusting people.'

I put the letter back in its envelope and returned it to my pocket.

'Have you asked anyone else about it Rob?'

'Only Bill Longman, her gardener come handyman. He thinks definitely she had the 'wind up' about something. And I presume the heart attack could have been brought on by something else other than high blood pressure, Eve?'

'Yes certainly a high stress situation at her age. I'm sorry I have not been more helpful' she said standing bringing the interview to a close. I was surprised how tall she was.

"Well thanks for seeing me Eve" I said a little disappointed at her abrupt end to the interview.

'Don't hesitate to contact me Rob if you need me.' With that I left the surgery and made my way back to Kantara.

Eight

The rest of the day I spent looking around Kantara. Picking up the telephone I listened to the dialling tone. Thought about phoning my parents and then rejected that course and replaced the receiver. It would all be too difficult to explain. For I did not even understand it.

All too soon I returned to Aunt Carolyn's journal for an answer.

'Allan-Cleary had gone, the bird had flown, and my discreet enquiries really got me nowhere. The trail had gone cold. People were sympathetic to me which drove me mad. But they saw no merit in the theories of conspiracy, and, as I began to go around in circles, began to avoid me.

Soon I doubted myself, and what had happened on that Troodos Mountain road. Perhaps my Father and Mike had got things wrong. Perhaps it was an accident after all.

However, finally, I did come across a snippet of information. A secretary at Government House spoke out of turn at a party which I gate-crashed. I told him I had some personal things for Allan-Cleary.

'Oh, he's back in London, at the Admiralty.'

With that information my resolve was to return to Britain. The Nicosia flat was returned to the Government. The bungalow at Kantara was locked up, it was mine now and I would miss it. In the heat of a Cypriot summer there was nowhere like it with the cool winds off the sea rustling amongst its pines and cypresses and the nightingales, such peace, would I ever know it again? In such a crazy world trying to tear itself apart.

However I did have one request to stay on Cyprus. An Army Lieutenant Druiff tried to recruit me; he described me as having outstanding knowledge of the island and linguistic skills, for the Special Operations Executive. To stay behind if the German's invaded to live in the mountains and help organise a guerrilla campaign.

I was flattered, it sounded exciting, but I declined sighting I wanted to go home. He was clearly disappointed but understood.

Before I left on a ship for Egypt I saw Kemal Faiz again. As always he was pleased to see me and pleased I was going home and looked forward to when I would return to Cyprus in happier times. We did not mention the accident again, but it lay like a great colossus between us. He apparently was moving on 'getting more involved with the war' was all he would say.

From Egypt I took ship to Cape Town, the Mediterranean was ablaze then with the Axis powers trying to knock Malta out of the war. From Cape Town I took another ship back to Britain.

On these voyages I had time to think as we dodged U-Boats, the more I thought the more I was convinced Dad and Mike had been right.

By spring 1942 I was back in London, staying with Liz my older sister who shared a flat in Belgravia with two other Wrens, all of whom worked with her at Naval Intelligence in the Admiralty.

Rather than blundering about with my suspicions, I let Liz believe Dad had died in an accident and I told her nothing of my Baby or Joe. But I did pump her by mentioning people on Cyprus which led to Allan-Cleary. He had been at rooms 38 and 39 Naval Intelligence for a month but had been moved on.

So the trail had gone cold again.'

There the first journal ended. Looking at my watch I was surprised to see it was almost midnight. Putting the journals under my pillows I went to bed and quickly to sleep.

The next morning was another beautiful spring day. Making breakfast I glanced at the second journal flicking through the pages. But I did not start reading; I needed to think about this.

'Hello Rob, sleep well' said Bill Longman, his head appearing around the back door.

'Yes thanks Bill want some breakfast?'

'Just tea.'

Pouring a mug for him he took it and made his way outside. Soon I heard the petrol lawn mower start.

The noise was not conducive to clearing my mind. So putting the journals in my jacket I decided to go for a long walk to think and clear my head. Telling Bill I would be back in an hour or two I set off for the beach.

The tide was out and I could walk right around to Seaton. Aimlessly I threw stones at the sea, and scrambled among the rocks.

Reaching Seaton I sat down using one of the *"Dragon's teeth"*, a chain of concrete obstacles put there in 1940 to hinder German invasion vehicles, as a back rest. Taking out my Aunt's journals I stared at the cover of the second volume. In her neat handwriting was written.

'Journal Two April 1942-August 1944.'

What should I do? Burn them, bury the past, after all it had happened a long time ago, over forty years, before I was born. Did I really have time for this?

A car drew up behind me, I took no notice.

'It's fine for some' came a familiar Canadian voice. Eve Reilly was sat behind the wheel of a red Triumph Spitfire with the hood down, she smiled broadly at me. Beside her in the passenger seat sat a lean swarthy looking man of about thirty, with intense black eyes.

'This is Ian' said Eve nodding in his direction. 'Ian, Rob Nicolson, remember I told you about his Aunt.'

'Sure good to meet you Rob' he said a thin smile crossing his face. He too had a mild I guessed Canadian accent.

'Morning Eve and Ian' I said leaning against the car's screen pillar, 'on your way to administer to the sick?', while getting a good view of Eve's thighs barely concealed by her short skirt.

'That's right; it's a lovely morning you could see for miles up on the Moor this morning. It reminded me of home.'

'You live on Bodmin Moor, that's a bit of a drive?'

'Yes up at Minions Rob, among the old tin mines. Not really much of drive, about fifteen miles I guess. Nothing compared to the distances we drive back home. Out for a walk Rob?'

'Yes trying to clear my head with the sea air.'

'Good idea' she beamed.

'Anyway, Bill's cutting the grass, bloody awful racket, I can't think with that going on. Think I might carry on along the coast toward Looe.'

'Well don't get caught out by the tide when it turns. Or else your walk might be a lot longer.'

With that she gunned the little car's engine and tore away in a shower of stones. I watched the little red car speed along the beach road then disappear over the headland around Rock's Nose toward Downderry.

I felt faintly put out with the presence of Ian, a boy friend, or husband. Both clearly came from the same place. But then I did not recall Eve wearing a wedding ring.

My walk took me further west along the beach, in the distance Looe the fishing port and Looe Island basked in the early morning sunshine. I imagined the little town's streets would soon be thronged with holiday makers.

After another half hour I turned back having reached no decision other than Bill, by now would have finished with the noisy lawnmower.

It took me about an hour to walk back along the road. At the village shop I stopped to pick up some things I had forgotten the day before. The husband served me this time but had little to say.

Reaching the end of the street before turning into the cul-de-sac I found the brown Ford parked again. I was sure it was the same car. It was empty this time; mentally I jotted down the registration number.

At Kantara it struck me something was odd before I went inside. The lawnmower had been left outside almost in mid strip as if Bill had been called away. Perhaps the mower had broken down; it was old way past its best, almost a vintage model.

Pushing the front door open I found Bill. He was lying face down in the corridor, in what medic's call the recovery position. But I had the distinct impression he would not be recovering. Dead bodies were not unfamiliar to me. I had seen several in my time. But most had died with a higher degree of violence than this, blown apart, or with gaping shrapnel holes or high velocity bullet wounds.

There was no pulse at his neck, but he was not yet cold. He had been dead perhaps an hour maybe a bit longer, I had been gone a little over two.

It took me a while to find the wound in his lower back. A knife wound up into the heart. You would need a long knife with a thin blade for that. This was a professional job. Bill had been taken totally by surprise. I stepped around the body and picked up the telephone and dialled 999 for the police.

There was no getting out of it now. Bill surely had died for the same reason as my Aunt, he had somehow known too much. I was in it now right up to my neck so to speak.

Nine

Two police constables arrived in a patrol car. One, the younger, was soon being sick in the garden.

'His first stiff?' I asked the older one.

'Yes that's right sir, only a few months out of Police College. You don't seem overly upset by this?'

'Only known Bill less than twenty four hours, and anyway have seen quite a few bodies in my time, most in a worse state than old Bill in there.'

I made them both a cup of tea, entering the kitchen by the back door to avoid the immediate crime scene. Soon after this their boss walked in Detective Inspector Montague, fortyish scruffy and dishevelled, looking like he had just got out of bed after a rough night. He spoke briefly to the constables then went and looked at Bill, after which he came and found me in the kitchen.

'Mr Nicolson you are the owner of the property?' said Montague, in a soft West Country accent after introducing himself.

'My Aunt' then I stopped myself. 'Sorry Inspector force of habit, yes I am now the owner of Kantara, my late Aunt Carolyn left me the bungalow.'

'She passed away not all that long ago I believe?'

'That's right a couple of months, I think.'

'So you did not know Bill Longman very well?'

'Hardly at all Inspector, although from what I gather Bill had worked for my Aunt for years.'

'Your Aunt was found dead here as well?'

'Yes by the local doctor Eve Reilly, heart attack she told me.'

'You know the Doctor?' said Montague raising an eyebrow.

'I made an appointment; asked her about my Aunt's death; as a matter of curiosity, saw her yesterday. You see it was a bit of a shock she left Kantara to me, for my family and me come to that. Wanted to know about her state of mind really', I felt it all sounded a bit hollow now. 'I told your constables about that suspicious Ford Cortina hanging about Inspector.'

'Yes the wooden tops told me we are looking into it. Nothing missing Mr Nicolson?'

'No not as far as I can tell.'

'Do you know any reason why anybody might murder Mr Longman?'

'No I don't think so Inspector.'

'So is that a yes or no Mr Nicolson?'

'No I don't' I said more decisively, telling myself that was the truth.

'You will have to come to the station in Liskeard Mr Nicolson to assist us with our inquiries and make a statement. The constables will take you there. I will have to wait on the experts from forensics.'

Thus I was taken away in a patrol car and soon ensconced in a drab interview room in Liskeard police station. Refreshment came in the shape of an awful cup of tea made with condensed milk. And I waited, the better part of three hours alone.

Standing looking out of the window onto the uninspiring spires and rooftops of Liskeard, I contemplated walking out, I was not under arrest, but if I did they probably would arrest me then. It was no good; I just had to be patient.

Finally Inspector Montague returned. Entering the room with another plain clothes officer he introduced as Detective Sergeant Doney, smarter than Montague although about the same age, mid forties.

'We have checked out your story Mr Nicolson which appears to be as you told us. More tea? Have they looked after you?'

'No thanks Inspector, I thought I had given up condensed milk when I left the service.'

'Yes horrible really, you are an ex-marine?'

'Former, Inspector, you're never an ex-marine with the corps.'

'Right I stand corrected' said Montague with irritation in his voice.

'Bit like the police I imagine once a copper etc' I said.

46

'You did nine years in the commandos' said Doney. 'Did unarmed combat, knife work I should think?'

'Yes on both counts, not so much knife work as you put it just an introduction really. I think you have been watching too many films sergeant', and left it there.

'Did you murder William Longman Mr Nicolson?' asked Montague.

'Don't be daft, I don't, I did not, know the man. And what is my motive, not to pay him for a few hours gardening work, come on you will have to do better than that.'

There was a knock at the door which interrupted proceedings. A WPC entered and whispered something to Montague.

'Be back in a moment Mr Nicolson' said Montague leaving me with Doney and the WPC.

'Mr Nicolson, if you would be good enough to give us your statement and finger prints so the forensics boys can discount you, you are free to go' said Montague, on his return in a few minutes. 'We have finished with the bungalow. Sergeant Doney will take your statement.'

The WPC and Doney left the room, the latter in search of some forms.

'If you should come across anything you think might help Mr Nicolson, here, you can get me on these numbers' he handed me his card.

'So I'm no longer the prime suspect?' I said taking the card.

'No that's right don't think you ever were either.'

I thought it a little odd, the card and all, why not just ring the station, but perhaps Montague liked the personal touch. And why the rapid change of tack, one minute trying to put me in the frame and quickly dropping that. But I was not going to pursue it with Montague; it would all be difficult to explain.

The boys in blue offered me a lift back to Downderry in a patrol car but I declined, I had had enough of their company, a taxi was fine.

Ten

There was hardly any evidence of the police presence at Kantara, and of course poor Bill was gone. It had certainly not been a violent murder, one thrust by someone who knew what he was doing and it was all over, and I was certain he must have known Bill.

My stomach was rumbling, but it was too early for a meal at the Inn-on-the-Shore and I had missed lunch, well it would not hurt me to wait. And goodness old Bill had only just been skewered that morning. I made myself some coffee. Taking the journals from my pocket I knew now the only way out of this mess was through them.

I opened journal number two *'April 1942-August 1944'* and began to read.

'April 16th London.

It is so good to be with Lizzy in London. Even with the blitz I feel alive again. She looks so smart in her Wrens uniform, and so lively I think secretly she is enjoying the war.

But I am making no progress in my investigation which is the purpose of this journal.

April 20th.

A bit of luck. They need secretaries at the Naval Intelligence Division with foreign languages. Having lived on Cyprus I fit the bill with good Greek and Turkish. Lizzy got me in, apparently that's how most people get into Intelligence by knowing somebody who knows somebody, seems a bit haphazard to me, even bizarre.

So I am working at Room 39 at Naval Intelligence in the Admiralty Building Whitehall. All I have done is signed the Official Secrets Act.

There is a lot of work which I find therapeutic, it helps me stand back and look at what happened with a fairly dispassionate eye.

May 2nd.

We handle thousands of agents and attaches worldwide, and the fight against the U-boats is desperate, and there are surveillance and special operations.

I realise I need to see Admiral John Godfrey the director, he works next door in Room 38, should be easy, just a wall away, but it might as well be a mile. He is so difficult to see alone, unnoticed, he is like God here. There he is behind his green baize door, summoning members of staff by the number of buzzes from the buzzer on his desk. I must find a way; I'll never get another chance like this.

To get into Naval Intelligence London you enter the Admiralty building by a door on the Mall behind the Captain Cook statue. Where I was escorted that first morning along a dark corridor the boots of the Marine sentry echoing off the walls. Then I'm booked in at the office opposite Room 39. This office was full of papers awaiting delivery I later learned in transit, it was also the home of the tea making facilities.

Room 39 is a high ceilinged, 19th century office like the rest, with cream painted walls and a black marble fireplace with iron coal scuttles. Three tall westerly windows facing the door look out onto the garden of No 10 Downing Street, the Foreign Office, St James Park Lake and the Guards Memorial and further to the left Horse Guards Parade. On the parade ground were the thick wires tethering several barrage balloons above.

There are ten naval officers working here, two male civilians, and four of us women secretaries, two Wrens and two civilian and now me. It is rather like any other office, telephones ringing, arguments, dictating and paper and 'docket's' thin cardboard folders held together by string everywhere. The Admiral's rule was strict, for when he was away and room 38 his domain was empty gossip would be the order of the day.

No RN officer of the group seemed to be in charge or able to impose discipline, they were known among us women as 'the zoo.' Yet Room 39 there is no doubt above all else is efficient.

To get past the baize door of Room 38 to see the Admiral you have to get past Lieutenant Commander Fleming who is the Admiral's personal assistant, his Mr Fix it. But he is cold and aloof, thin, handsome in a way, but unapproachable. Mind you he treats everybody with the same contempt be it a General or Tea Lady.

Edward Merrett is the Admiral's secretary perhaps I will approach him. I must act quickly who knows what damage Allan-Cleary might be doing. Mind you I doubt I should really be keeping this journal under these circumstances.

May 5th.

Today I plucked up courage and waited for Merrett on Horse Guards. At first I think he thought I was trying to pick him up. But I blurted it all out. Once I started I had to finish.

To tell the truth I felt a fool, it all sounded hollow and mean. It all seems far-fetched here, away from Cyprus, here where a real war is going on and people are dying every day.

I must keep in my mind Joe, and Dad, and Mike Foote and my un-born baby, all dead because of Richard Peter Allan-Cleary, and how many others have been his victims?

Saturday June 20th.

I am still waiting for Merrett to come back to me. Sometimes I find myself looking toward his desk. Even though I catch his eye sometimes, there is no spark, he does not look away as if I were an embarrassment, he holds my glance with no acknowledgement. Churchill is in Washington meeting FDR and Allan-Cleary is there too, how much damage will he cause?

Monday July 6th.

Lieutenant Commander Ian Fleming met me rather like I had Merrett, he was waiting for me, and we sat on a bench in the early morning summer sun. He chain smoked.

'Carolyn you have conveyed some suspicions about RP Allan-Cleary to Mr Merrett. Tell me about them, take your time. But tell me everything.'

So I relayed the entire story to Fleming. He listened without interrupting. Eventually I finished, rather feebly I thought.

'I knew Allan-Cleary at school' he told me.

That made me think I was sunk. The old boy network would come into play, the old school tie and everything, they were above suspicion.

But Ian went on. 'Mike Foote I knew briefly, he was no fool. You are also right about the Rommel Raid it should have been cancelled. And it was RP who should have stopped it. Possibly it might have been an oversight. Another thing we believe, somehow Rommel got wind of 'Operation Crusader' and from a source in Cairo. Leave it with me I will dig a bit more. Say nothing about this to anyone else. Well there it is.' And that was the end of our conversation. You always knew that with Ian when he used those words. 'Well there it is'. Today Ian seemed almost human to me.

Tuesday August 4ᵗʰ.

Commander Fleming saw me again today, in private, he said;

'I'm not sure about RP, Carolyn; but I think you might be onto something. He's in Washington at the moment so we will bring him home. Washington is too important if he is a double. We are drafting him to Western Approaches' Plymouth where we can keep a better eye on him. Would you like that job?' he asked, turning those pale blue eyes on me that seem to examine your soul.

I could hardly believe it and I stammered something like 'yes please'. As if I was being asked out to dinner. I have no idea what 'keeping an eye on him' might entail.

Tuesday August 18ᵗʰ.

Interview with Admiral Godfrey today, he gave me quite a grilling. Commander Fleming was there as well. I don't think the Admiral swallowed a word of it he is inscrutable, but they cannot take the risk.

'We have withdrawn RP from Washington, our relationship with the US is vital and it's hard to observe him there at arm's length. So he's coming back to Plymouth, promoted to Commodore, which should keep his suspicions under control. Carolyn, you will watch

him down at Guz, keep your distance though he could be a nasty customer, and if he rumbles you, it could be dangerous. Report to Fleming here, if he does cotton on get out quickly, otherwise just observe him the Admiral told me.

I asked why they did not just arrest him.

'If he is a spy he may be more useful to us in his present condition; we may be able to feed him false information. By the way the Allan-Cleary's have a place in Cornwall, what's the place called Ian?'

'Gweebarra sir between Kingsand and Cremyll on the Cornish side of Plymouth Sound. Named after Gweebarra Bay, county Donegal in the Irish Republic, the Allan-Cleary's have an estate there as well.'

'That's it then Carolyn, good luck, and be careful' said the Admiral rising he shook my hand and the interview was over.

Admiral Godfrey hardly seemed the irascible ogre everybody thinks he is. Mind you some of his questions about men friends were a bit personal.

But on the other hand I am now an agent of Naval Intelligence. I wonder if the pay is any better perhaps I should have asked that.

31st August 1942.

I have lodgings in Plymouth near the Hoe. The city has suffered badly from bombing there are great blackened gaps where buildings used to be. I am a secretary at Western Approaches HQ, not a very good one. It is an underground complex out at Hamoaze. Have not seen RP yet.

Monday September 7th 1942.

Now an agent better put proper dates down and everything, wish I had had a little training for this job I feel totally inadequate.

Saw RP today I was a little worried he might recognise me but no, a lot of women work here both civilian and service. And I have changed my appearance since Cyprus my hair is much longer, and in a different style. And I wear glasses; I don't need them they are just plain glass.

He looked just the same to me. Think I will try and get over to Cornwall just to have a look at Gweebarra, the Allan-Cleary family seat. Must not get too close though, but from what I have learned so far, merely office gossip really, he does not stay there often.

RP gives the impression of working really hard, he is at his desk sometimes sixteen hours a day. I suppose he is working hard for his Nazi Masters.

Saturday September 19th 1942.

My day off, went to Cremyll on the Cornish side of the sound today by passenger ferry and walked toward Kingsand, beautiful day even if autumn is in the air. Motive not just a walk but to get a look at Gweebarra.

American officers are now billeted at Mount Edgcumbe. They are working with us in the war against the U-boats and most welcome. One a naval officer stopped in a jeep and offered me a ride, but I declined saying I was enjoying my walk. "As you please miss" he said and drove off with a cheery wave.

It was about two miles to Gweebarra, I ventured down the drive toward the house which is hidden from the road. My heart was racing; if anyone had spotted me I would say I was lost. It is an imposing house with tall chimneys overlooking the sea toward Plymouth Sound and the breakwater. Its gardens and lawns reach almost to the sea. In a small boat anybody could land there easily, say from a submarine on the tiny beach. Or is this my imagination working overtime?

The house appeared deserted, no smoke from any of its chimneys, which are tall like gun barrels pointing at the sky. No sign of movement. I stayed in the fringe of the trees that line the drive largely out of sight. I did not have the nerve to move closer.

Tuesday September 29th 1942.

Still cannot pin anything on RP other than him being a hard working officer. Perhaps I am wrong. After all the Admiral had his doubts.

The buzz around the HQ is there are battles going on in Russia and Egypt that just might turn the course of the war.

Thursday October 29th 1942.

Have been working at the Royal Marine Barracks Stonehouse today, I was told I was needed to translate some material. But it was a ruse to meet my contact, superior Commander Frank Slocum SIS head in Cornwall.

Told him I had nothing to report as such and was beginning to doubt my initial suspicions.

'Oh no Carolyn, our masters in London are pretty sure you are on the right track. And RP is hardly likely to advertise the fact he is a spy' said Slocum.

'Why not arrest him then Commander? I asked.

'Well, I don't know old Fleming keeps his cards close to his chest. But I believe they hope to feed him false information, hoping his masters might act on it, it's a tricky thing to pull off'.

He gave me a direct contact telephone number to him and I return to the Hamoaze tomorrow".

The light was beginning to fade I put the journal down, got up and had a bath. I wanted to wash the air away, the air of death, and the feel of the police station from me.

Washed and in clean clothes, taking the journals I walked down to the beach and watched the sun sinking in the west beyond Looe Island. I made my way to the Inn-on-the-Shore and ordered a simple supper of fish and chips at the bar taking a pint of bitter to a table in the corner I was the only customer.

I found it hardly credible that my Aunt had known Ian Fleming, or even more startling she had worked in the field for naval intelligence. My Aunt that sent you thoughtful presents like the latest Dinky Toy, or a welcome Postal Order. My theory about them meeting in the publishing world was clearly way off the mark.

A woman that was surrounded by unpretentious things and lived a simple life by the sea. An aunt who took us exploring amongst the rocks looking for crabs and shells.

Big shells in which if you placed them to your ear you could listen to the sound of the sea. An aunt who sat on the beach watching over us as we played in the water. How we misjudge people I thought.

'Hello again' said the chubby landlady, I had passed the time of day with before, when she brought my meal.

'Did not realise you were Miss Thompson's relative. Must have been a shock to you finding Bill Longman like that?'

'Yes it was.'

'Police got any idea who did it?'

'No they seem as baffled as me in all this.'

I saw her eyes glance down at the journals lying on the table. 'Refill?' she said pointing at my empty pint glass.

'Yes thanks' I said, and she moved away with my glass to the bar. I doubted Downderry had had so much excitement for many years.

Eleven

Quickly I wolfed down my supper, I had not realised how hungry I was. And I was keen to return to the journals, but waited until I had finished my meal and could concentrate totally on them, and my fresh pint had arrived.

'Saturday November 7th 1942.

Everybody taken by surprise with the landings in Vichy-French North Africa of American troops, 'Operation Torch', and Rommel on the run as well, the tide is turning. RP shows no emotion.

Sunday November 15th 1942.

Not at work today. Church bells have been ringing for the desert victory of El Alamein. The Russians advancing too at Stalingrad.

Thursday December 3rd 1942.

Saw Commander Slocum at Stonehouse barracks again today. He is sending me to the village of Downderry, in Cornwall; there have been some reports of odd goings on there that might bear on RP. Downderry is not far from Gweebarra about ten miles to the west and fairly remote.

Saturday December 5th 1942.

Took the train to St.Germans and a taxi from there to Downderry, which was actually a grocers' delivery van. Downderry, a coastal village with radar aerials of the 'chain home' system running along the beach between the sea and village, I met a Captain Pearce there commander of the local Home Guard. He was a little concerned SIS had sent a woman to investigate and a young one at that.

But he was keen to tell me what had happened. A German aircraft had come in low two days before. He was sure it was a Junkers 88, and insisted I write that down. As if me a mere slip of a girl could not remember such detail.

'Captain could the pilot have been disorientated, or merely looking for an easy target instead of risking the flak over Plymouth?' I asked.

'Could have been Miss. But we have had reports someone was signalling to the enemy aircraft guiding him to hit Downderry. Would not have been a local or Cornish person,' he added gruffly.

'No I'm sure about that' I reassured him. 'But why Downderry?'

The Captain had no explanation for that question.

'Could it have been a distraction, were your men out on duty that night?'

'Yes from Seaton to Portwrinkle'.

'And you called them in after the raid?'

'Well yes, after the signalling report. We had to try and catch the bugger.'

Which left the beaches uncovered a rather obvious ruse; there was little doubt in my mind someone had come ashore that night the raid merely to cover them. The aircraft had missed the radar station at the eastern end of Downderry and the radar aerials were intact.

I reassured Captain Pearce he had done the right thing, he was a nice old boy really.

Who had done the signalling? That was the question, was RP off duty on that day? It would be easy to check. But surely it would not be him he would be too important. Was there an enemy ring or group operating here?

I questioned a few other Home guard members, all terribly keen. William Longman, giant of a man, was sure it was true somebody had been signalling with a powerful torch up on the ridge line above the village, one of the stick of bombs had landed up there, they had all fallen on fields way off the mark.

He had been at Rock's Nose look-out post, the other side of the ridge overlooking Seaton beach. The aircraft had flown right over him he could feel the beat of the engines then it had turned sharply out to sea.

I stayed the night at the Eddystone Hotel at Seaton.
Sunday December 6th 1942.

Met Bill Longman again he took me up to the fields above Seaton where we found a fresh bomb crater. But no evidence of the signalling or signaller.

'Why bring the aircraft right down on your head?' I said.

'Perhaps they were not much good at it, all done in a hurry. Perhaps the pilot was not up to it, flying toward what probably looks like a cliff to him' suggested Bill.

Bill took me over to Maker Heights to an anti aircraft battery above Kingsand, not far from Gweebarra, I had to hang on for dear life on the back of his motor bike. I was scared stiff, but exhilarated as well. I have not been so close to a man since Joe, but there is something about Bill I like.

Now Carolyn, concentrate, you're behaving like a schoolgirl. I spoke to the CO of the battery. They had seen the plane coming over the sea too late to engage it, it was too low, and if they had fired they might have hit the villages of Kingsand or Cawsand. They saw no signalling. And were busy anyway engaging enemy aircraft over Plymouth.

Tuesday December 8th 1942.

Returned to Plymouth, saw Commander Slocum and made my report. At last we have something to go on RP was off duty on the night in question at Gweebarra that puts him right in the frame. But who has come ashore to warrant such a cover operation? Must be pretty important as well for RP to be active and risk his cover.'

Closing the journal I glanced up, I could feel somebody watching me. The landlady was nearby clearing a table.

'Another drink?' she asked, indicating my empty glass 'closing time soon.'

Yes thanks I'll have another pint.'

'You were asking about the Allan-Cleary's earlier in the week. Martin, the son, was in tonight. Funny thing he asked about Bill Longman and your Aunt came up. Can't imagine he knew either one of them, not in his social circle.'

'Did he ask about me?'

'Not really, as I recall, although you know how it is, I pointed you out.'

'You did?' my blood ran cold, was I now in the frame.

'Not gossiping, people merely interested' she said defensively. Perhaps she had noticed the look on my face.

I followed her up to the bar to collect my pint I wanted to get back to Kantara and back to the journals.

'Mine's a pint as well' announced a North American voice from behind me. It was Ian, Eve Reilly's husband, boy-friend or whatever.

'Oh! Hello, another pint for my friend' I said to the landlady. Pints in hand we moved away to a vacant table.

'Not holding you up Rob?'

'No it's fine' I said even though he was. He lit a cigarette, offering me one from a pack of Marlboro which I refused.

'Wise man no good for you and that's a fact. Eve's always on my case to give up. Mind you staying at that bungalow, your Aunt's old place is positively bad for your health bodies everywhere I hear, what's it called?'

'Kantara.'

'Kantara, odd name.'

I explained it to him, why I don't know it had nothing to do with him, but he seemed a good listener, changing the subject with, 'So where's Eve, on overtime?'

'Doctor's you know what they are like, or maybe you don't, but that sister of mine boy is she devoted to medicine.'

'Oh! Sister' I said 'I thought you and she?'

'Were an item, that's a joke, no we are half siblings same father different mothers. I'm just visiting from Canada over here to cover the Miner's Strike.' With that he took out his wallet, which I could not help but notice bulged with money, he extracted a card he slid across the table, which told me he was a reporter for a Toronto paper.

'Keep it Rob might come in handy.' With that he got up clutching the empty glasses.

'Pint's it is' he said before I could refuse he was heading for the bar.

Ian came back with a tray with two pints, and two whisky chasers that looked like doubles.

'Eve's a bit of a looker, her mother was a stunner as you can tell I got the mongrel blood. You interested in Eve Rob?' he asked lighting another cigarette.

'Well I don't...' I said stumbling for words.

'Off course you don't me here playing cupid, but any hot-blooded male. Give it a go Rob is my advice. Think she likes you. Never know your luck.' With that he slapped me on the back and laughed loudly.

'Have you two been discussing me then?'

'Well you did come up after the last murder. Bill Longman wasn't it. Just remember I'm a newspaper man always snooping for a good story.'

I took a good gulp of my beer; I was beginning to feel full up. And Ian's chain smoking made me feel heady.

'What do you think of the strike then, have you been up north yet?'

'Sure in Yorkshire, bitter business. Poor devils are being crushed by all the power of the state, don't stand a chance.'

'Is that how you see it, but seems the Union leaders have picked a fight?'

'Trying to protect their members way of life, but we will not argue. My job is to report the facts and what happens not opinions.'

Ian had finished his drinks I was lagging behind.

'Another chaser a night cap on me' he said raising his empty whisky tumbler?'

'No thanks Ian' I said finishing my pint. 'I'm off to my bed it's been a long day.'

'Of course the state has been hard on you too.'

'Hard on me! No I don't think so. With all these bodies turning up in what amounts to my house they are bound to try and see if I fit the frame.'

'If you take my advice I would book in a hotel. There is something about that place Kantara, they do rooms here I believe?'

I drained the whisky and got up. 'I'm too old to be afraid of things that go bump in the night. But it's been interesting Ian.'

'Yes good on you man' he said rising. We shook hands. 'Don't let them stitch you up Rob. And I'll put in a word with Eve for you before I go north tomorrow and then home.'

He grinned at me through yellow teeth as I left. I heard his loud voice in the background. 'Another double whisky landlady and none of that Scottish stuff let's have some of the Irish, did I see some Jameson up on your shelf?'

I was not entirely sure at that time whether I liked Ian Reilly or not.

Outside the night was still and clear the stars bright in the sky, as if you could reach up and touch them. I waited in the shadow of the pub holding my breath waiting for my head to clear. Trying to detect anybody waiting for me, but there was no movement. No suspicious sound, other than the odd movement of dishes and clearing up sounds coming from the pub.

Descending the steps from the pub to the beach I walked east which brought me to Beach Road and Kantara. I had half expected to see a parked brown Ford Cortina but there were no vehicles to be seen.

Twelve

Inside Kantara I carefully locked the doors and windows. I reflected on Ian's advice not to stay on in the bungalow, and laughed at it. He might be afraid of things that go bump in the night I was not. I had been trained to treat darkness as my friend. Making a coffee to help clear my head I took Aunt Carolyn's journals to bed to read on, she had now reached 1943.

'Friday 1ˢᵗ January 1943.

It's a new year. I worked on Christmas day, could not help thinking of Daddy and past Christmas's on Cyprus, but it does not do to dwell on it. RP did not work.

Nothing has come of my time spent at Downderry. It is a frustrating business this intelligence work, perhaps I'm not really cut out for it.

Sunday 24ᵗʰ January 1943.

Casablanca conference today. Italy must be the next target once Jerry is cleared from North Africa, no secrets there, everybody knows that. RP still going about his work seemingly normally, keeping his masters informed no doubt, how does he do it? From where?

Wednesday 10ᵗʰ February 1943.

Cold day today my flat is freezing. Great joy, something of a breakthrough. One of the girls at the registry told me RP has been looking at 'Most Secret' messages regarding a flight to Algeria from RAF St.Mawgan some high ranking Free French officers and SOE agents are due to fly out. That's not within his remit, has he slipped up signing for these documents, given us a clue. But what does he know?

I saw RP watching me today, or was it one of the other girls? He was reading a file on top of a filing cabinet, kept glancing in my direction, I could feel his eyes on me, has he rumbled me?

I kept getting the feeling someone followed me home. But I saw no one am I suffering from paranoia? I think it is time to contact Commander Slocum.

Friday 12th February 1943.

Commander Slocum came to see me at home, is that a risk? What if I'm being watched? They have put Gweebarra under observation, using some Auxiliary Units, secret part time army I have never heard of them, they are setting up hides to watch the house. Slocum told me to watch RP more closely. Also a Royal Marine Major is arriving at the Hamoaze who is a field agent for NI to give me back up, some muscle as he put it. My I do feel important.

But what are they waiting for, why don't they move?

Tuesday 16th February 1943.

Major David Cox has arrived. Made himself known to me. Real tough soldier, but a dear, met me in the ladies of all places. He was on the Dieppe Raid, has a pronounced limp and a freshly healed scar running the length of his right cheek, we lost a lot of good men there. I'm glad he's here.

Thursday 4th March 1943.

Called to Stonehouse for translation work, Commander Slocum and Major Cox there, at last we are moving.

NI has got someone on the inside of this group based on Gweebarra. We are going to move in on them get the whole 'parcel' of them. Saturday at dawn, it's like a military operation.

'Carolyn would you like to come, to be in at the death so to speak, mind you it could get sticky' said Slocum.

'Gosh' was my reply; I can't believe I said that.

'It was you who alerted us so you should be, David here will be in charge.'

'Thank you Commander, yes, I would like to be there, just to see his face, as long as I don't get in your way.'

'No problem eh David.'

'None at all' said the Major 'ever handled a pistol Carolyn?' He said to me.

Saturday 6th March 1943.

It was before light as we began moving toward Gweebarra. The night was still, the sky clear. The frost crunched underneath our feet as we moved through fields. There were dark faces and dark figures around me. I stayed close to Major Cox who was carrying a sub machine gun. I could feel my heart beating; it seemed as if it was hammering against my chest and my breath coming in gasps.

The house came into view, big and grey, imposing with its little forest of chimneys. We stopped on the edge of the drive in the cover of trees.

All was quiet; Major Cox spoke in whispers, slowly waiting until we all understood. His men were divided into three groups. Two men were sent to knobble the vehicles, to cut off that escape. Three men went to cover the rear of the house. There was another road block at the top of the drive of regular soldiers. 'Friendly forces' as Major Cox said in his military jargon.

That left five of us to approach the house across the lawn on the seaward side and to cut off that avenue of escape, although there was no evidence of any boats. This is the real front of the house, with a wonderful view of the sea and Plymouth Sound, Cox, Slocum, myself, and two others, one of which, I could hardly believe when I saw him, was Bill Longman. He grinned at me through a blackened face his teeth starkly white, and helped me black up.

So Bill was in the Auxiliary Army, he was no ordinary Home Guard, although they wore the same uniform.

We started across the lawn weapons drawn. I was trembling, not from the cold either. Major Cox had shown me how to use the pistol, it was loaded, safety on, but I had not fired it, and did not want to. I stayed close to the Major the others fanned out either side of him.

It was just growing light; we left a trail of foot prints in the grass of the frosty lawn. There was a sea mist hanging above the shore line and stretching a few yards out to sea. The sea was flat calm it looked so beautiful so tranquil.

Then, suddenly up ahead there was a shout, a young woman burst from French windows in a nightdress, onto the wide veranda stretching the length of the house, and began to run toward us, she scampered down the flight of steps leading down to the lawn. When a man burst from the same French windows he raised his hand, a shot cracked out, it seemed so loud, and she pitched forward. Bill had moved out to the side trying to get a shot away as she was in the line of fire. As she fell a fusillade of fire broke out from us. I saw Bill fire his rifle kneeling, the man was hit, smashed back into the house. My pistol remained silent, I was a mere spectator frozen in time, and I did not even point it in the general direction it remained pointing at the ground.

'Come on follow me' shouted Major Cox, and we ran across the lawn up the stairs into the house they went passing through the French windows shattered by our fire. I waited outside heard another window smash and saw Bill climb into another room through that window.

Slocum had stopped beside the crumpled form of the woman, she was dead, he covered the body so tenderly with his long bridge coat.

When I went inside the drawing room I found the dead man had been thrown grotesquely like a rag doll back into the room, his face a pulpy mess where one bullet had hit him.

They caught RP in the kitchen, burning documents in the range, and dragged him handcuffed into the drawing room. He looked right at me, his cold eyes burning into me. All he said was 'So' recognising me at last and nodded his head, a half sneering smile crossing his face.

I said nothing, I was frozen. Bill put a reassuring hand on my arm and steered me away into another room, a sitting room by the look of it.

'You were great Carolyn' he said and produced a hip flask. 'Bit early I know' he said handing me the chrome flask.

The brandy made me cough but it was good.

Commander Slocum entered, with him was Commander Ian Fleming I had no idea he was coming down to be in at the death, it showed how important Allan-Cleary was to them. 'Is that some of the hard stuff corporal?' said Slocum to Bill.

'Sure sir, want a nip?' he said handing him the flask. Slocum's nip was a good swallow.

'That's good man' he said wiping his lips with the back of his hand. He handed the flask on to Fleming.

'The woman?' I asked.

'One of ours, dead I'm sorry to say they had just rumbled her brave girl. What a mess.'

'But we have RP' I encouraged.

'Not only him, at least three others in the house. The housekeeper is Irish and two others we think are Germans. They have perfect English. Unfortunately, one code named 'White Fang' an Abwehr agent has flown the nest if he was ever here. But a good result just don't like losing any of our people. Sometimes we treat this like a game but this is a war, best not to forget that.'

'That's right Frank' said Ian to Slocum, they did not move away from me including me in their conversation. I was one of them. Ian went on ; 'Our boys will give them a good grilling. And well done Carolyn. Thank goodness he never got near Room 13 in the Citadel or the Ultra decodes.'

Ian motioned to me to follow him outside, he offered me a cigarette which I declined he lit one himself, using his cigarette holder it was one of those Morlands with the three gold bands he had made on special order.

I don't think anybody I knew ever really got to understand Ian fully, knew what made him tick there were so many layers to him. He had a certain roguish charm, he was fit and lean, a bit like an athlete a boxer with his crooked broken nose.

'Do you like the work Carolyn' he asked, 'if so you could come back to London with me.'

Ian had a bit of reputation then as a rake, I wondered if he was trying to pick me up, but at the same time I did not doubt the offer as totally professional.

'This was personal for me Ian, I think I would prefer to stay in Plymouth until it's over if I would be useful to Frank.'

He nodded. 'As you wish Carolyn I'm sure you will have a part to play down here' with that he squeezed my shoulder. 'Well there it is Carolyn' and he moved back into the house.

Part of my reason for wishing to stay in Plymouth was that it had been good to meet Bill again; I think I might like to live in Downderry when the war is over. The end of my journal is close, perhaps this is it.

Saturday July 17th 1943.

A footnote really, I have not heard much since that Saturday morning in March.

Commander Slocum told me RP and the others would be interrogated for some time probably months, and then will be executed for 'High Treason'. They did not cancel the aircraft to Algeria from St.Mawgan, but it never made it.

There were crates of gold on board as well as the passengers. The plane was observed, some miles off Watergate Bay on the North Cornish Coast, as it exploded and crashed into the sea, Slocum told me shrugging his shoulders.

He thought perhaps a victim of 'White Fang' the agent had completely slipped their net. Picked up by a U-boat perhaps or had he got away to southern Ireland? But the landings in Sicily had gone well, that was the most important thing.

Tuesday 7th September 1943.

The Allies have landed in Italy, Mussolini the Duce has fallen. And my life as an agent for Naval Intelligence is over. Admiral Godfrey sent me a letter of thanks for my efforts. Explaining 'Operation Mincemeat' a deception of great importance took precedence and could not be compromised which was one reason why things might have seemed to move so slowly. And I guessed that was the reason why that young woman had died and those people in the Warwick Bomber had died in a ball of fire over the sea, to save our lads landing on Sicily.

I continue my work as a translator at the Hamoaze, but I think somehow, life will never be quite the same again.

I closed the book. 'Well Aunt Carolyn' I said out loud. My Aunt had seen action, and it looked like she might have been sweet on Bill Longman. Was he the reason she had come to live in Downderry?

My watch indicated it was past one am, my eyes were tired. But I looked at the cover of the third journal. The same type of school exercise book, on the cover was written Volume III 1947- the second date was not filled in like the others had been. I was intrigued obviously things had not ended with Volume II after all, but it could wait until tomorrow.

I could hardly keep my eyes open. I put it with the others on the bed side cabinet switched out the light and sleep quickly enveloped me.

Thirteen

It was dark when I woke. Pitch black, something was wrong. My nose and mouth were covered I was forced to breath something mephitic somehow familiar but not familiar. My struggles were futile my shoulders and arms were pinned by strong hands my legs constricted by the bed clothes. I could not move. I could make out shadows and hear rapid breathing other than my own. Then I was falling spiralling away, I tried to hang on, to stay awake, but I continued falling, falling backward falling into darkness.

Cold woke me, I felt stiff, and my head ached and swam. I thought, as my head slowly cleared, I did drink quite a bit last night but surely not that much.

Slowly I became aware of my surroundings. There was no bedding on me that was odd, even stranger I found I was dressed. Feeling with my hands the mattress was bare, no sheets nothing, which was wrong. Badly wrong, and the bed frame was iron, which told me for certain this was not my Aunt's bed which had a feather mattress and wooden frame.

There was no trace of light, no difference in shadow. It felt and smelt damp and dank, but I could move. Slowly I sat up waited for my head to stop swimming, fighting back a wave of nausea. There were shoes on my feet, through them I felt a hard floor surface, reaching down I felt cold damp stone, no carpet not like the bedroom at Kantara.

My watch was still on my wrist thankfully it was luminous, it read 9.20, but 9.20 when, was it 21.20? Surely not I thought, I did not feel particularly keen to empty my bladder.

Sitting still for five minutes I listened, listened to nothing, I could hear no sound at all, no creaking no slight movement usual in all houses. One thing was certain I was not in Kantara.

My head had cleared although it still ached and I felt sick. It came back to me slowly; I had struggled last night or in the early hours against someone. Probably more than one person, what the hell was going on? I told myself to stay calm.

Standing up I swayed a little waited to gain my balance and then slowly groped forward like a blind man, hands outstretched. In three steps my hands encountered a cold stone wall. Turning back to the bed my shoes felt odd, loose. Back sitting on the bed I found my shoes had no laces that told me one thing for certain I was a prisoner, and in a big building.

Darkness had never bothered me even as a child, the bogey man was no nemesis for me. One reason was nowhere is usually pitch dark. But this place other than my friendly watch was dark like the grave. I felt my pulse at my wrist it was strong if a little fast comforting that, at least I was pretty sure I was still alive. Still functioning if not running on all cylinders.

I got up again movement was reassuring and groping with my hands slowly explored the room. It did not take me long to find an iron cell like door studded with large rivets, cold, very cold to the touch. Finally I found what I was looking for, a switch, a light switch. Not a plastic rocker one, but a metal round one I tried it and suddenly was bathed in light from a single bulb in the roof encased in a thick wire mesh fitting. My eyes quickly adjusted, the room was bare other than for the one piece of furniture, an iron bed with a bare smelly damp mattress.

Sitting on the bed again I took stock of my situation. I was dressed in my own clothes, trousers nothing in the pockets, shirt, and jumper, no underwear, shoes without laces no socks.

I guessed I had left my watch on last night and my captors had missed it or more likely did not care that I had it, which meant what, nothing I could fathom.

Who the hell were my captors, and why, after all, I had only asked a few questions surely not enough to get up somebody's nose? It must have something to do with RP, his son perhaps, if so he had a long reach and help but why? Then I thought I bet I came here in the back of a brown Ford Cortina. And where was here? The place had a military air about it. It was almost, somehow, in a way, familiar.

Fourteen

It was so obvious, but something you take for granted. I sat there for over an hour before I tried it. The door had one of those flat sliding bolts to lock it; I guessed there was padlock or some other locking mechanism on the other side. Not really thinking about it when I was taking a short stroll around my cell, beginning to feel like the Count of Monte Cristo, I tried it.

The bolt slid back with no resistance whatever, I pulled the door open and looked out into a dark empty corridor. It was damp with small water puddles on the rough hewn floor. The walls were roughly finished granite blocks, with no attempt at decoration like the painted police cells.

Saying goodbye to my cell I moved out into the corridor. Which way to go? I stood listening for a minute or more, still nothing other than the occasional drip of water from the roof.

My instinct was to turn right, was that because I was right handed I reasoned? So I turned left.

The light from the open cell helped me for a while. There were other light fittings on the corridor roof but I decided against trying to light it up, it would be a beacon to announce my presence. Telling anyone who was interested I had left the cell. Eventually I got to a right angled turn. I had passed several other doors like my cell had, but I left them alone trying to keep sound to a minimum., as I turned something scurried away a rat no doubt. But what caught my attention was light up ahead strangely subdued but no doubt light. Flooding down from above, natural light from the outside world and not far away.

I moved cautiously toward it. Reaching where it cast its shadow a flight of steps led up from the bowels where I stood. I passed up through two other levels, the steps were well cut and even. Whoever built this place had made a good job of it. The light became brighter. Finally, cautiously, I emerged outside into moonlight, overhead the stars were out, a clear night. So it was 21:30, but which day? How long had I been unconscious?

I had emerged at one edge of the centre of a Victorian Fort, like Tregantle, but not Tregantle. The centre area was grassed, a path running around the outside between the grass and walls of the fort.

I made my way toward the main entrance not cutting across the middle, but keeping to the shadows cast by the walls. Stay in cover as much as possible it was automatic. My training drummed into me over years told me this might be safer.

Even via this route it did not take long to find the way out. The main entrance was open. I crossed a narrow bridge over a dry moat.

Outside on a tarmac turning area was parked a brown Ford Cortina and a Land Rover. I thought about trying to take a vehicle, but decided against it, too noisy, it would alert my captors even though the place felt deserted. The fort was surrounded by trees, making it almost invisible with its low profile to the casual observer. Down below, to the east were lights, civilisation, help, I made my way toward them.

Reaching the edge of the trees on my left, to the right were open fields. I saw up ahead two shadows, human shadows, moving in the moonlight coming my way. Coming toward the fort, I darted back into the trees crouching down in the cover, completely concealed.

They passed within feet of me, I could see the glow of their cigarettes and smell the acrid tobacco smoke, and hear the low murmur of their voices as they talked. There was little doubt in my mind they were two of my captors but I could not make out their faces.

I waited until they were well clear, and must have been within the fort before I moved on. Running without shoe laces proved almost impossible, the best I could manage was a fast awkward walk. Passing some farm buildings a dog began to bark, but I took no notice, hurrying on.

The pitted grey track turned into a tarmac road. I took off my shoes and carried them I could move much faster in bare feet, although the occasional stone made me wince.

At the end of the lane I turned left toward nearby lights, passing the signpost that informed me this was the village of Antony.

The Ring o' Bell's pub was well lit up, probably it was from there my captors, the two men, had been returning from to the fort. A ruckus sing-song was belting out from the pub. I could not risk entering the hostelry for help; there might be others of my recent captors having a drink. But surely there could not be that many, I was not that important. Finally I dismissed the idea; I needed to put distance between me and the immediate area. I needed to think clearly.

There was a bicycle, a push-bike, leaning against the pub wall. It was not chained or locked I wheeled it silently away. I could hardly believe my luck. I wanted to kiss the God of those on the run.

At the bottom of the road past the Ring o' Bell's I came to a signposted T Junction. Right was Torpoint, I knew the town across the Tamar River from Plymouth it had a ferry service, left Sheviock, St Germans ultimately Liskeard and Detective Inspector Montagu.

I turned left and was soon pedalling frantically something I could manage even with ill-fitting shoes. This direction would allow me to disappear into the hinterland of Cornwall. Right would have meant me backed up against the river. With no aid in sight, neither option was particularly appealing.

From the fort I had noticed in the distance a TV transmitting mast, its line of red warning lights pointing at the heavens. That was where Eve lived, what was the village called? I could not remember. It was somewhere on the edge of Bodmin Moor. An area smaller than Dartmoor yet big enough to disappear into, I would be hard to find. But it was close to that mast, a long shot, I hardly knew her. But Ian had hinted at her interest in me, had to hope it was fairly strong. For I could not go back to Kantara not yet; I needed a bolt-hole, somewhere to rest up. The police would only mean questions none of which I knew the answers to, I needed time to think. Help from them was definitely not welcome at this point.

Fifteen

It was years since I had ridden a push-bike but it was true you never forget. I proceeded without lights the moonlight lit my way. How long I wondered would it be before I was missed. There was little use worrying about that, all I could do was put distance between them and me whoever they were.

Soon I was labouring uphill into the village of Sheviock. But I did not have to get off to walk. The odd car speeding toward me was not so much of a problem, other than being blinded by the lights.

It was more like Russian roulette with those coming up behind, who might knock me off, and run over me. Mind you, I was giving the drivers little chance with no lights. But from that direction it could be my captors.

I was badly out of condition, wheezing like an old steam engine. Several pounds had been added to my weight since leaving the corps and exercise had been problematic. I was light headed too, probably dehydrated, it was hours, and perhaps days since any liquid had passed my lips, and most of that had been alcohol, and I hadn't eaten anything come to that. Not the best preparation for such exertion.

The car that hit the bike knocking me off came fast from behind in a blaze of lights and a roaring engine. It sent me spinning head over heels, luckily I landed in a forest of nettles that broke my fall and stung me all over. I dragged myself up cursing "bloody drivers" and moaned about the loss of a shoe which was impossible to find amongst the nettles.

Thankfully the bike was still in one piece nothing was buckled, it had only been a glancing blow. The car never made any attempt to stop, probably never even saw me.

At the hamlet of Polbathic I turned off the main road, onto a B road, still heading in the general direction of the TV mast. Barely an hour had passed since leaving the fort.

From then on at the approach of lights I would dive into the hedge or a gateway waiting for the vehicle to pass, though on these smaller roads cars were few and far between.

The TV mast lights guided me on. It took them hours to get closer. My feet became a mass of cuts and blisters.

Through Tideford I passed and Blunts and St Ive, all small villages some only hamlets. All were quiet with only odd lights showing from houses. At last leaving St Ive the mast looked closer, and a signpost had Minions on it. 'That's it" I said out loud. 'That's where Eve lives.'

Knowing where I was going, and getting closer lifted my spirits. However it was still mostly uphill and I knew I was reaching the end of my stamina. I was running on empty. But finally, after climbing the steep hill from Upton Cross, passing old mine workings marked by the stark ruins of the engine houses, I arrived in Minions on the edge of Bodmin Moor. I stopped at the Post Office. Nearby was the TV mast, looking huge now like a giant spear pointing at the heavens, so close as if I could reach out and touch it, perhaps half a mile away.

The trouble was now where did Eve live? I had no real idea. The village was not that big perhaps fifty dwellings in all but forty-nine too many for me.

From the Post Office I could see nothing obvious. But what was obvious? I limped over to the Cheesewring Pub, glancing down a lane running beside the pub I saw a red Triumph Spitfire parked. It had to be Eve's surely, the hood was up.

I picked the small cottage opposite the car, walked up the path leaving the bike in the garden, and banged on the door.

Eve must have been a light sleeper; for it was only the second series of knocks that woke her, it was four in the morning. An upstairs window creaked open Eve's head appeared.

'Who the hell is it?' she called out.

'Rob, Eve, Rob Nicolson.'

'Rob, buddy are you crazy, do you know what time it is?'

'Sorry but I've had an accident.'

'Oh! Hang on I'll be right down.'

And she was soon opening the front door, blinding me with the powerful beam of a torch, perhaps under the circumstances a wise thing for a woman alone to do.

'My God Rob, what happened to you? You look awful.'

Sixteen

Opening the door Eve was dressed in a big fluffy pink dressing gown with a rabbit logo on it, her hair ruffled having just come from her bed.

I was practically out on my feet and staggered past her into the cottage. Eve pushed me down a narrow corridor to the kitchen at the back. It was an extension to the original two up two down miner's cottage. I slumped into a chair at the kitchen table relieved to sit down. My legs felt like jelly and for several minutes would not stop shaking and relax.

'What happened to you Rob?'

'Drink please Eve' I croaked, through dry cracked lips. She bought me a glass of tap water from the sink which I quickly downed and then another.

'When was the last time you ate anything Rob?'

'No idea Eve, what day is it?'

'Day?' said Eve surprised, 'why it's Tuesday, well no its Wednesday now, Wednesday morning.'

'Sunday then, was the last time I ate or drank anything.'

'O.K.' said Eve taking the empty glass to the fridge and filling it with milk. 'Slowly Rob, drink this slowly' and placed it on the table.

'My feet hurt Eve.'

'I should think so, you have got blood over the kitchen floor, let's have a look.' She knelt down before me and examined the soles of my feet, and then looked up at me. 'They are cut and bruised some nasty looking blisters too, dirty, but no need for stitches.'

Eve got up and left me for a moment. Soon I could hear water running upstairs, back she came. 'This way Rob I have a bath running' and she helped me up the stairs.

'No need to be shy seen hundreds of guys in the buff' and she helped me strip off and then climb into the bath which made my feet sting for a moment, but it was wonderful to sink slowly into the warm water. By the smell of it the water was laced with disinfectant, she helped me wash, tackling my feet carefully.

'I hope you don't do this with all your patients Eve?'

'No Rob and you are not my patient. Now come on Rob spill the beans let's hear what happened to you?'

Trying to concentrate I told her the story from the beginning, including meeting her and Ian her brother, while she helped me out of the bath and dried me. I sat on the toilet wrapped in a big bath towel while she dressed my feet. Removing with tweezers some pieces of embedded grit, and then put some cool antiseptic cream on them, finally dressing them in some large loose socks. She did not interrupt me until I had finished.

'Into bed young man' she helped me into the only bedroom and into her bed.

'Eve I didn't know you cared.'

'I don't think you pose me any problems in that department in your present state. And anyway it's getting light; I would have to get up soon as I have the morning surgery.'

Eve disappeared downstairs again, while I sank into the luxury of that double bed that smelt so pleasurably of her, and was still warm from her body.

'Here we are' said Eve returning with two pills and another glass of milk. 'Take these, just mild sedatives to help you relax and sleep.'

I did not argue with that.

'Who do you think these gangsters are?' she asked sitting on the edge of the bed, watching me sit up to take the pills.

'I presume they must be henchmen of the Allan-Cleary's, they are a bit like the local Mafia perhaps. Something like that. Or that's the impression the locals have given me. Perhaps Mafia is a bit too strong a word.'

'Well they do seem to act with impunity' said Eve, sounding rather doubtful. 'Tell you what I'll take a look at your place in Downderry, see if I can get some clothes for you.'

'Be careful, they have murdered one person for certain, maybe two. And it's the first place they would expect me to return to. They will be watching the place. Funny Ian warned me off staying at Kantara.'

'I still think your Aunt died of a heart attack. Don't worry' she said combing my hair 'I won't take any risks. I have to see some patients in Passmore Edwards Hospital in Liskeard this afternoon so I will not be back until late afternoon.'

'Perhaps I should ring the police, that Inspector Montague?'

'Well it's up to you, but don't you feel even they might be involved in some way, perhaps corrupted even?'

'The British Police, never thought of that' I said yawning 'no you have been watching too many films.'

Eve gently pushed me back onto the pillows. "Look wait until I get back, then see how the land lies. Take it easy buddy boy there is plenty to eat in the ice box".

These were the last words I heard before welcomed sleep engulfed me in its warm folds.

Seventeen

Waking up, light was flooding the bedroom even through the curtains. It took me a few moments to recall where I was. I had a dull headache. The bedside alarm clock told me it was nearly twelve noon. It was good to lay there relaxing for a few moments, listening to the normal sounds around me. The trouble was I soon began thinking and then going in circles, so I got up.

Other than my feet, which were sore, and my fuzzy head, I felt in pretty good shape, and hobbled to the bathroom. Returning, I wrapped myself in Eve's fluffy dressing gown which was hanging on the back of the bedroom door, it was a bit short in the arms and not really me, but was warm.

In the kitchen I found the fridge well stocked and I began making myself a good breakfast, eggs, bacon, mushrooms, toast, fruit juice, and coffee. As I found out the intricate workings of the electric cooker, I noticed a radio on the window sill and switched it on, catching the news.

'Talks between the NUM President Arthur Scargill and Chairman of the Coal Board Ian MacGregor broke down after only an hour this morning.'

Then Scargill was on the radio speaking with his rapid shrill voice, that MacGregor was *'a butcher sent to destroy the industry.'*

So they got on famously I thought, although perhaps Arthur had a point. Funny MacGregor was Canadian like Eve and Ian; I would have to ask her what she thought of him. The presenter went on to local news, one item grabbed my attention.

'The police in a statement say inquiries continue into the Downderry murder, and they are making progress.'

I laughed at that one. Progress, they did not have a clue, or did they? Somehow I got the feeling Eve did not quite trust them. Probably she might have had some run in with the authorities in the past, clouded her judgement.

Breakfast was a treat and I made some extra toast which I had with honey. In the lounge I switched on the TV and lay on the settee, within minutes I was asleep again.

'It does not suit you' said Eve shaking me awake.

'Oh hello' I said rubbing my eyes. 'What's that you were saying?'

'My dressing gown, not your style Rob.'

'No perhaps not, nice and warm though.'

'Got your clothes Rob' she indicated my holdall. Inside were shoes as well as my wallet, she had brought my corduroy jacket as well.

'Thanks Eve any sign of the enemy?'

'No all quiet I went round the back which was still open, saw how they got in. Cut out some glass near the back door lent in and unlocked it. You want a bolt there. Pretty professional, a neat job whoever did it?'

'The diaries?'

'No sign of them, I had a good look around.'

'No they should have been in the main bedroom where I was sleeping.'

'Better have a look at your feet Rob?' She sat on the settee and examined them closely. 'Looking much better, you're a quick healer.' She worked some more cream into them gently.

'Wait till that dries, I'm pretty bushed, going to have a bath.'

I watched some mindless TV quiz for a few minutes then got up and switched off the set. I dressed putting on some clean socks, but did not try my shoes. Everything in my wallet was complete.

Eve was soon back looking fresh in jeans and a tight sweater. 'Fancy going next door for a meal.' she said.

'Next door?'

'The pub the Cheesewring, mainly steaks and the like.'

'Yes great, I'll pay' which was the least I could do.

'Well I will not object to that, ten minutes and they will be open.'

Eighteen

The Cheesewring was warm, snug and inviting. We sat in a corner, at that time, early evening, the pub was largely deserted with only two customers at the bar talking quietly.

We ate our way through a large steak each, in silence. I had a pudding to follow, while Eve savoured her wine.

She broke the silence. 'So Rob, what's the plan?'

'As I see it I have two options. See the cops, or go home and forget all about it.'

'Forget what Rob?'

'Exactly, I still don't know what I'm facing so going home is not an option.'

'However' it came to me like a flash of light. 'There are cops and cops; I have another turn on that.'

'Another turn, I did not quite grab that one as it ran past me, try me again?'

'Sorry Eve you have no idea what I'm talking about. I have an old oppo, friend, from my days in the Marines, we joined up together, went to our first unit together after training. Taffy Harris, Kevin Harris, he's still in the Corps, and lives down here; Yelverton up in Devon as far as I know. Anyway that's where I sent his Christmas card last year. I think I can find his house, although I left my address book at home. With any luck he won't be away.'

'So how is this Taffy Kevin Harris going to help you?'

'Kevin Harris, Taff, Taffy is just a term for a Welshman; like the Irish are Mick's the Scottish Jock's.'

'Oh they are, are they.'

'No, listen Eve, Kevin is in the RMP, Royal Marines Police. He went into that branch after his first unit. He might well be able to find out if there is anything going on, unofficially, last I heard he was in the SIB, Special Investigations Branch.'

'Sounds good to me, someone you can trust. Yelverton, that's over toward Dartmoor isn't it?'

'That's right, between Tavistock and Plymouth.'

'I have the evening surgery tomorrow I could run you over there in the morning.'

'That's great Eve, and then I would be out of your hair.'

'Well that would be a bonus. That's not to say I have not found your company' she hesitated struggling to find the right word 'what shall we say, absorbing.'

We both laughed at that one. By now the pub had filled up quite a bit even for a week day, and it was dark outside. I went up to the bar and ordered another pint for myself and black coffee for Eve. There I could not help overhearing a heated discussion about the Miners Strike. I overheard, 'That Ian MacGregor, Thatcher brought him in to do a hatchet job on the coal board like he did on the steel industry.'

'He's a foreigner too, bloody Canadian isn't he?' said someone else.

Taking the drinks back to our table I asked Eve. 'What do you think of our poor country consumed by this strike, it's almost like Civil War, and your country man MacGregor's coming in for some stick?'

Eve took a sip of her coffee. 'One crime in this country for certain you can't make coffee that's for sure. On the strike, by the way MacGregor is Scottish American not Canadian the one at the coal board that is. Mind you the government seem tyrannical; it's almost as if they picked this fight, the image comes across of a Police State.

Ian went back up north for a while before he went home. Says it was pretty grim. One of his headlines was *'Heroic Miners doomed in their struggle.'* He got part of a brick in the face, hit him on the cheek had to go to A&E up there. Down here in sleepy Cornwall you don't see it, but if I was a doctor in South Yorkshire who knows

85

what I might feel. Big Brother 1984 remember that book, think he had something.'

'Is that how you see it, I never thought of it that way?'

'Rob, you, the Brit's, have been fighting a civil war for years in Ireland, an occupied country, your first colony.'

'Civil War, no that's a sectarian war, between Catholics and Protestants, I did three tours over there keeping them apart.'

'But if the British left Ireland?'

'Yes there would be civil war then and the majority don't want us to leave.'

'The majority of what?' said Eve turning away; a man emerged from the bar crowd beside her rattling a tin.

'Support for striking miner's families' he said rattling his tin again.

'Here' said Eve stuffing a ten pound note into the tin.

'Thank you' said the man 'that's generous miss.'

I put some change into the tin the man sniffed at me with a curt 'thanks.'

Eve smiled at me. 'I'm always on the side of the underdog, the oppressed. See I'm on your side. Anyway it's time to get some rest, doctors orders.'

'Ah! If you put it like that I will not argue.'

Eve insisted I share her big double bed rather than sleep on the settee. Although no hanky panky was stipulated. Still I went out like a light as soon as my head touched the pillow, feeling secure, for the first time since I had arrived in Cornwall, in that small moorland cottage.

Nineteen

We set off early the next morning after breakfast of cereals, fruit juice and coffee. I was told cereals would be good for me after all the meat I had eaten. Doctor's orders again.

It was a fine clear morning, just a little mist hanging in the valley floors that were laid out below us like a map. Minions or Caradon Hill where the TV mast stood stark against the sky was one of the highest points on Bodmin Moor.

Eve took the road to Upton Cross and onward through the lanes via B roads toward the main Launceston-Callington road which would take us onward over the border to Devon. She drove well if a bit too fast for my liking.

'What colour did you say that car was, the one your kidnappers used?' asked Eve.

'Brown, brown Ford Cortina why?' I said, having been day dreaming admiring the country side, the hedgerows were alive with colourful flowers.

'There's a brown car been keeping station with us through the lanes I think he's following us.'

I watched behind using the passenger side wing mirror and glancing over my shoulder a few times.

'I think you are right Eve, lose him in Callington easy.'

In minutes we were in the small town, which Eve drove around several times. In and out of the car park around some large housing estates with so many changes of direction we were confident we had lost them. With no Cortina in sight we took the Tavistock road toward the Devon border.

However out on a long straight skirting Kit Hill toward St Ann's Chapel, I spotted him again having taken station, hanging back, trying to keep cars between us, but no doubt.

'He's there again' I said 'keeping cars between us trying to hide but still there.'

'There must be a bug on you' said Eve.

'No I don't think so' but I turned my holdall inside out searching, and examined my shoes minutely which made me wince taking them off and putting them back on in the confines of the car.

'Nothing, maybe it's on the car. They might have spotted you going into Kantara yesterday. They would have been expecting me to go back there. Put two and two together followed you which led to me. Turn off right up ahead' I indicated 'if we can lose them for long enough in the lanes we may be able to spot the bug.'

Eve shot off right hardly slowing down, cutting across the front of an oncoming bus with feet to spare, I could see the driver braking violently and smell burning rubber. As I looked back over my shoulder he was shaking his fist at us.

The Triumph Spitfire sped through Norris Green and then into Metherell, both small hamlets, Eve turned into a farm lane entrance screened by trees bringing the car to a skidding halt and we were both out quickly.

It did not take long. Eve found it on the inside of the rear bumper. I got it off, the magnet was quite powerful. We kept looking for a while in case there were two but found nothing.

'You are going to throw it away Rob?'

'No I have a job for this little feller let's get going.'

In Harrowbarrow, near the post office I got Eve to stop. I leapt out as inconspicuously as possible and sauntered over toward a parked Morris Minor saloon. There was no one about. Bending down pretending to adjust my shoe lace I attached the bug to the inside of the front bumper.

Back in the Triumph, Eve sped away. 'That was a good idea' she laughed, 'life with you is certainly not dull.'

Presently we rejoined the main road, and settled down to a more sensible speed; hopefully my ruse had taken care of those on our trail.

In a few miles we crossed the River Tamar, brown fast flowing between steep green hills, via the narrow road bridge at Gunnislake, the border between Cornwall and Devon. I had half feared to see the Cortina waiting here, that might have been if they had rumbled the fact we had switched the bug, or there was a second on the Triumph, otherwise they were following a Moggy Minor around Cornwall.

'Eve, even over here I think it best if we stick to the B roads.'

'O.K.' she nodded 'you're the boss.'

Soon the little sports car was heading south on a largely deserted B road. Dropping down into a valley past woods, and plantations of pines, we crossed the narrow Denham Bridge over the Tavy River, tributary of the Tamar. The Tavy had formed this valley thousands of years before. Climbing the other side of the valley Eve had to use the lower gears in the gearbox frequently. We passed through the sleepy village of Buckland Monachorum.

'I know this place' I said.

'Hope so' said Eve 'for I have no idea where we are.'

'Buckland Monachorum, an oppo lays here buried in the churchyard, he was killed in the Falklands war.'

I shook off the melancholy feeling for I could hardly conceive it was only two years ago. 'Not far now Eve' I said. Famous last words I got us lost against the barrier of Roborough Downs. I had walked this way many times before on exercises. Walked being the important word, but there was no way through for the car. It took us an hour to find the main road again at Roborough, from which we could head back north toward Yelverton.

At Yelverton finding Meavy Rise on the Meavy road was a lot easier, a collection of a dozen modern bungalows in a cul-de-sac, a scene of domestic normality. Taff Harris's place was easy to spot among them for there was a big bike, a Yamaha 500 parked on the drive. Kevin Harris was a motor bike nut.

Twenty

'As I live and breathe R.N.Nicolson, Rob, where did you spring from?' cried Kevin Harris. He then engulfed me in a bone crushing bear hug with his six foot six frame. He had lost more of his hair since the last time I had seen him on Green Beach at San Carlos Water in the Falklands.

My tag R.N. had been given to me in my training days, when a drill sergeant had used it. *'R.N. Nicolson, you have joined the wrong service with initials like that, my gawd and looking at the state of you, you might make a good matlow.'*

'Got a bird in tow as well' continued Kevin running his eyes over Eve.

Eve kept close to me; no doubt wishing to avoid one of Kevin's all embracing bone crushing hugs.

The three of us were soon sat around the kitchen table with steaming cups of coffee, and an open tin of biscuits.

My story did not sound any better with another re-telling. Kevin pondered it for a few moments.

'Hoped you could put me up Kev?'

"No problem pal, got the spare room to get your head down, but this yarn of yours it's, it's' he searched for a description 'it's like some cheap thriller. What do you think Doctor Eve, had the old lady, R.N's Aunt, lost her marbles?'

'Not as far as I'm concerned. Although you must realise I did not know the lady that well.'

'Hmm' commented Kevin. 'Well there is something we can do. Check on Fort Scraesdon, whether it's being used at present. It still belongs to the MOD. That by the sound of it is where they held you.'

'I think, if you do not mind Rob and Kevin', said Eve 'I would like to be on my way, things I need to do.'

'Of course' I said 'Eve you have been great to a virtual stranger.' I went out with her to the car, while Kevin made some phone calls.

'Keep in touch' said Eve kissing me on the cheek. I was disappointed to see her drive away. She had been the best thing about this whole business. She had rapidly become a kindred spirit. But as she had pointed out, if there was a second bug on the car, she would draw them away. I was not happy about that, but there was little I could do, perhaps later I could tie up with Eve again, it would be good to get my feet under her table.

Back in the bungalow on Meavy Rise, Kevin was still on the phone I could hear his murmured voice in the hall.

'Scraesdon Fort' said Kevin returning 'is out of bounds for any training at the moment.'

'Which means what?'

'Which means my old mucker, that the sneaky beaky's are probably using it.'

'What the SBS or SAS?'

'Something like that or more likely SIS or MI5.'

'You're telling me I was kidnapped by the Government?'

'No, I'm not, all I'm telling you is the people who might be using Scraesdon Fort at the moment. It does not prove anything.'

I thought, there lies the view of a policeman.

I spent the night in Kevin and his beautiful petite Maltese born wife Agatha's spare room; they were as different as chalk and cheese those two.

I don't think she was over the moon at my unexpected presence. Especially as the evening turned into a drinking night, during which we consumed most of Kevin's beer supply and a bottle of Bacardi rum, while talking over old times boring her silly, that was why no doubt she went to bed early.

Agatha went off to work the next morning, she worked as a receptionist in a big Plymouth hotel. She wished me well before she left, which I took as a hint she did not expect to find me there on her return. Kevin told me he had not told the 'little lady' anything about my plight. Just that I was down in Cornwall sorting my Aunt's affairs and had just looked him up to say *'hello.'*

Kevin rang into Stonehouse Barracks where he worked and managed to swop his duty with another RMP Sergeant so that he could devote the day to me. 'I think the best thing you can do R.N. is go back over to Cornwall and see how the land lies now. I'll take you over on the bike.'

That prospect was not all that appealing to me. Not just the going back, I knew I had no real choice on that one. Rather it was the prospect of a ride on the back of Kevin's bike, I knew what that meant, a white knuckle ride. And with a thick head after all the drinking the night before it was not to be savoured.

It was not quite as bad as I had thought, remembering past rides with Taff. Most of the trip was through Plymouth in the rush hour crossing the Tamar, near the naval dockyard, via the Torpoint Ferry to Cornwall. From the ferry we gazed over the expanses of Plymouth Sound, the scene of many leavings and returning in the Corps. There were some naval ships riding at anchor in the Sound, one an aircraft carrier, another an assault ship we watched landing craft moving in and out of its flooded dock at the stern. The sea air helped clear my head.

From the small town of Torpoint it was a short ride out to Antony. Kevin had no real chance to use the power of the 500 Yamaha. We rode up the lane to Scraesdon Fort. There were no vehicles parked outside. It looked deserted.

Ignoring the signs that said 'Keep Out' and 'MOD Property out of bounds, Strictly Private Property', we went inside, it was deserted.

Riding back down the lane we came across the farmer, who lived nearby, on his tractor and trailer. He told us the Fort had been in use over the last few days. But they had packed up and gone now. An 'Odd Lot' was his only comment.

From Tregantle Fort at the top of the hill overlooking the sea we took the coast road. Passing through Crafthole and onto Downderry, the weather was clear again with an onshore breeze.

Arriving back at Kantara the bungalow was the same as Eve had found it the day before. I showed Kevin where they had broken in, whoever they were. And then Aunt Carolyn's letter which was all I had from her now.

'What do you think I should do now Kevin?'

'If you take my advice man, I should see that civvy copper what's he called?'

'Inspector Montague.'

'That's the one, tell him what you have told me and see what he has to say. And start enjoying your legacy, you're a man of means now R.N.'

I thanked him for his advice, and said I would think it over, but I was not enthusiastic, somehow it did not seem the right course to me. The local plods had got nowhere finding Bill Longman's murderer. We talked about the old days again, and then Kevin was gone on his way home. As a policeman himself, albeit a military RMP, I should have known he would advise the official route.

I watched him ride away, although it was good to feel he was only a call away. Inside Kantara I started on the roll top desk sorting the paperwork.

Trying to lose myself in a mundane task, my Aunt kept all sorts of things, receipts and bills going back years, in fact decades.

The phone ringing after an hour interrupted me, by which time I had a large pile of things to ditch or burn.

Picking up the receiver I said 'Hello.'

'Robin I thought you were going to stay in touch' it was Mother; I groaned inwardly, I had quite forgotten all about the family. 'You have been down there for days, well not there. I have phoned several times. What is going on, where have you been?'

'There is a lot to sort out' I prevaricated 'but I'm getting there.'

'What do you mean? You're hiding something?' I could hear the irritation in her voice.

'Aunt Carolyn wanted me to sort things out; we have to respect her wishes' I said weakly.

'You, why you, I don't understand, I'm coming down there as soon as I can.'

'Look Mum, there is nothing you can do, it's a bit complicated. Just be patient another couple of days, by Monday, it will be clear. Just stay put until then.'

'I don't know, it's not right, I'll see what your Aunt Karen thinks. Ring me tomorrow Robin, you hear me, promise me?'

'Yes Mum, I promise' I said with my fingers crossed.

'If you don't I'll be on the next train. Are you getting enough to eat Robin, I know what you young men are like, probably drinking enough.'

'I'm fine Mum.'

'O.K. we will speak tomorrow.'

'Bye Mum.'

'Bye Robin.'

I put the phone down and thought that was a close one. Thinking about it I picked up the phone again and unscrewed the receiver end, inside was a bug; I screwed it back on leaving the bug there. So that's why the phone had been connected so quickly. That had been put there by people with clout, but not the Allan-Cleary's. Not by any local toughs. But why?

After that a drink became vital. So I made my way along the beach to the Inn-on-the-Shore for lunch and a think.

Twenty-One

'Back again, not having seen you for a couple of days thought you might have gone home' said the landlady at the Inn-on-the-Shore.

Was there too much surprise in her voice, or was I getting paranoid myself? Imagining things that were not there. The bar was deserted.

'No, a lot to do with my Aunt's stuff.'

'That's right you did tell me.'

The thinking process had begun on the way to the pub. Churning things over, things had been happening around me, and to me, but I had not instigated events, other than turning up like a bad penny in Downderry. If my mere turning up had caused this many ripples, what would happen if I took the initiative. If I grabbed the bull by the horns, could be risky I thought, but what the hell.

'Martin Allan-Cleary been in yet?' I asked taking a sip of my beer still standing at the bar.

'No bit early for him, but he comes in most days.'

'Does his father come in?'

'Old Peter no, goodness me no' she smiled 'not for years I believe he's in a wheel chair now. Sad really but it comes to most of us, illness and the like unless you die young of course. They say he had a rough time in the war, in the navy I think. Do you know the family then?'

'Not really, but my Aunt, Carolyn Thompson did know Peter, the father, pretty well during the war.'

'I could let Martin know when he comes in if you like.'

'No that's alright I'll catch up with him sometime.'

I ordered some sandwiches, and took my drink to a table sitting down to wait. I was banking on the landlady being something of a gossip.

Thus Martin Allan-Cleary would hear I was looking for him. Would he rise to the bait? If him, and his hench men had been responsible for my kidnap he would come looking, no doubt about that, but somehow that theory did not add up.

The landlady soon brought over the sandwiches. 'See you are limping a bit?'

'Yes had a fall, twisted my ankle, nothing much really just a bit sore.'

'You want to take more water with it' she went away laughing to serve a customer who had just come in.

Over an hour passed with no sign of Martin Allan-Cleary, it was obvious he was not coming in for a lunch time drink today.

Leaving I took a short walk around the village; my feet were getting easier now. In the Spar Shop I got a few things and laid more bait there. Apparently he called there for cigarettes sometimes. I had the feeling the shop was as much the voice of Downderry as a grocers'.

Back at Kantara, Eve's Triumph was parked outside. As I walked up the path she appeared around the side of the bungalow.

'Ah there you are Rob, thought you might be around the back when I got no reply. Feet must be getting better; you seem to be walking easier. Still I will take a look.'

'What without an appointment, what would the dragon say at the surgery?'

'Come on inside' she smiled 'you're lucky getting the personal service.'

In the lounge after taking my shoes and socks off I lay on a settee while Eve examined my feet, taking particular care over the soles.

'They are healing fine Rob, but no marathons. Come on then spill the beans' she said pushing my legs off the settee to sit beside me 'don't leave me in suspense.'

She smelt wonderful and looked fresh. 'About what?' I teased her.

'Come on, what did Kevin have to say?'

'Typical policeman really, although he's a good buddy to have, he advised going to the cops.'

'But you don't see it like that?'

'No I think I need to confront the Allan-Cleary's, make things happen to them and not me.'

Eve nodded. 'I think you are right but you need to be careful, I don't want to keep patching you up or having to sign any more death certificates.'

'I have started laying the lines already' I told her what I had done at the pub and shop. 'We will see if they take the bait.'

Behind Eve I saw through the window a blue Land Rover pull up behind her Triumph, out climbed a bandy overweight man dressed in shorts I guessed this might be who I had been fishing for.

'My I did not think I would get a bite as quick as all that I'm impressed with the Downderry grapevine.' I hurriedly put my socks and shoes back on.

The big man stood puffing at the front door a smile on his large bulbous face. Dressed in khaki shorts and a similar colour shirt which were dirty and dishevelled, on his feet he wore open toed sandals with no socks, his body odour was strong. He looked anything but the rich local landowner I had taken him for, with his fingers in all sorts of pies.

'Heard you wanted to see me" he said extending his hand. "Martin Allan-Cleary, old boy at your service.'

I took the hand, the shake was firm. Was this the shake of a traitor I thought?

Although he was the son of a traitor, did that make him a traitor, was he in on it, did he know his father's background? I had to guess he did. By the look of him he was in his fifties, doubtful then he would have served in World War Two.

'Yes, I'm Robin Nicolson good of you to come around, come in please' I led him into the lounge.

'I'll be on my way Rob' said Eve nodding to Martin Allan-Cleary as we entered the room.

'As you like Eve, thanks for checking on me I'll see you around.'

'OK Rob, all part of the service, keep in touch.' Eve picked up her bag and saw herself out.

'Wish I had a doc like that, bit of a looker great tits, mine's an old goat' said Martin Allan-Cleary.

Could this man be out to get me, could he have murdered Bill Longman in such an efficient calculating manner? I somehow doubted it.

'I would like to see your father Peter. He knew my late aunt, Carolyn Thompson.' I handed him a photo of my aunt. 'She died a few weeks ago.'

Martin examined the photo and then handed it back, his light hearted air seemed to have evaporated. But he made no comment.

'They knew each other during the war', I continued 'I think they met on Cyprus first in 1941 or 1942?'

'Not much point seeing Pop's, losing his marbles would not remember back that far, confined to a wheel chair old man.'

'My aunt thought he was a traitor. He was arrested in 1943 as I understand it. Yet here in 1984 I find he's free, no doubt drawing an old age pension, living off the fat of the land.

I think it got my aunt all riled up. Was it a shock to him to learn my aunt was here? Ready to reveal him to the press.'

Martin's bulbous head had sunk into his shoulders his eyes darted around the room, did he wonder if anybody else was here hiding. But I maintained the attack.

'If you know about it you must be covering up for him. Did you, or some of your hench men, steal her diaries from here. Try to rough me up a bit?'

'I would be careful what you say Nicolson. The best thing you can do is go back where you came from and let sleeping dogs lie. You don't know what you're getting into.'

So that confirmed it, there was something in Aunt Carolyn's story. 'No Allan-Cleary I'm not going to do that, I'm after him, justice for my aunt, and the others he betrayed. I'm no old lady to be pushed around.'

Martin brushed past me for the door, he turned there.

'I warn you Nicolson, leave it alone' and then he was gone.

Twenty-Two

That night I stayed in at Kantara. Ate the last of my potatoes' and eggs with some corn beef, watching my aunt's black and white TV. There was still a battle of words, and of bricks, bottles, truncheons, and fists going on in the Miners Strike. Also the news showed the marching season was in full swing in Northern Ireland with the Republican events producing the usual hackneyed rhetoric, masked supporters and marchers in paramilitary garb. Loyalist parades attracted a good turnout featuring the bands with bowler hatted Orange men marching, under ancient banners. I had seen it all before. In my day they often descended into riots. It was different now from my tours in the nineteen seventies. Today the lads were facing a numerically smaller, but much more sophisticated enemy. The IRA was more selective more accomplished and still had pots of money.

Before going to bed I made sure the doors and windows were securely locked and closed. And I laid some basic booby traps an intruder would trip over in the dark, pots pans that sort of thing which should give me a good warning. However I spent a restless night.

It was a lovely morning when I woke with a fuzzy head, the result of too much broken sleep and boozy nights. I wandered around the garden with my coffee, it took me back to what always seemed long sultry summers of childhood, if they were really that good other than in my memory was debateable.

In the village I soon learned that a bus ran along the coast from Looe to Cremyll which was opposite Plymouth. I caught it.

The bus chugged its way to Portwrinkle, along the wide sandy expanses of Whitsand Bay favoured by surfers and on to the twin villages of Kingsand and Cawsand.

The driver dropped me opposite the drive to Gweebarra. I would knock at the front door see what response I got to that. The direct approach was often the best.

A grey drive wound down from the main road to the house of Gweebarra, with its many chimneys visible above a screen of trees and huge rhododendrons with blood red flowers, in the distance beyond, the sun's rays were sparkling on the sea turning it silver in places.

Grass grew in the centre of the drive I had reached about the half way point when two men appeared in the drive in front of me they must have come through a gap in the hedge. They awaited my approach.

'Hello friend' said one as I drew near. Over his arm rested a broken shot gun I could see cartridges in both barrels ready to be snapped shut. 'Lost your way or something?' he continued 'this is private property no trespassers.'

I carried on up to them stopping close so as I could get a good look, both were thick set, obviously muscle men, I did not recognise them. The one without the gun was striking the head of a heavy walking stick rhythmically into the palm of one hand, trying to convey an air of menace.

'I want to see Peter Allan-Cleary.'

'Got an appointment?' said the one with the gun.

'Of course not.'

'Name?'

I told them, the one with the stick turned away a few paces and spoke into a walkie talkie. All I could hear was the murmur of his voice.

'Sorry pal' he said turning back 'not at home.'

'A likely story' I said. The two goons just stood there leering at me.

There was no choice, I turned back and retraced my steps. I heard them follow me at a distance, no doubt reporting to their masters when I was off the property.

Back at the main road I walked the couple of miles to Cremyll, opposite the Royal William Naval Yard in Plymouth. There was a bus stop there from which I could catch a bus back to Downderry.

The Cremyll Arms soon opened and I had a pint sitting outside in the spring sunshine, watching the river traffic. So I thought I would have to take a more indirect approach to Gweebarra if I wanted to get inside. But I was determined to get in there at the Allan-Cleary's, it was my only alternative.

It was late afternoon by the time I got back to Downderry and Kantara. I phoned home then, telling mother all was going well I would be home by the beginning of the next week probably Tuesday. By then all should be sorted. I could tell she was not happy with that, she was itching to get down here. I had the feeling Dad had calmed her down, and I could hear his restraining voice in my mind *'let the boy handle it.'* The last thing I wanted was relatives down here now getting in the way; I would have to force things along but how.

Twenty Three

Most of the food at Kantara I had eaten, so that evening meant another short walk to The Inn-on-the-Shore, which had the added bonus, perhaps, that I would be able to annoy Martin Allan-Cleary if he turned up, which I somehow doubted. Being a Saturday night the place was quite busy. I did not take much notice of the people there, other than keeping an eye out for Martin.

I stayed until near closing time, not drinking much. I was beginning to value the benefit of a clear head.

It was a clear night and I took the beach route back to Kantara. I heard some people behind me but thought little of it guessing it was probably a favourite haunt of courting couples until;

'Hey Nicolson' somebody called out. Stopping and turning I found three youths facing me, hardly out of their teens.

'Martin asked us to sort you out mate' said the smallest of the three, although he had a stocky build.

'He did, did he? You think you can do it, don't think he will have paid you enough, I suggest you go home now and get your nappies changed.' I backed around, they followed me before they realised I had the sea wall at my back. They could only come at me from the front then.

It was all over in two or three minutes. My assailants were weak in the art of self defence and dirty street fighting.

Unlike myself who had taken on the Commando maxim *'fight dirty'*, and had been in a few punch-ups, from Union Street in Plymouth, to the Gutt in Malta.

The stocky one led the charge but the others hung back. I caught stocky a good blow on the chin which staggered him back. And then launched a kick at one of the others, a tall thin youth with greasy long hair, it connected well with his soft groin; he doubled up. The third a chubby roly poly sort took to his heels. But stocky came in again now alone; he caught me a glancing blow across my cheek bone. But I was on him gouging with my fingers my nails clawing toward his eyes, while bringing a knee up into his belly. That was enough for him; he broke and followed his mates.

I waited by the wall regaining my breath and composure in case they returned. But no, they were gone and had had enough.

Back at Kantara I made up an ice pack for my face but knew I would have a shiner in the morning.

In bed I thought over the events of the day. My plan had worked, I had their attention, and I had stirred up the Allan-Cleary's. However I was glad my assailants had not been the two up at Gweebarra they were more accomplished, I suspected, in the art of fighting rather than the pimply youths. It was just another attempt to scare me off. However it did raise the question why had they not used the two men?

About two in the morning I was woken up by a vehicle drawing up outside. What now I thought? But I was ready for them.

I was up quickly taking a peek out the front window. It was not what I had expected, it was a police car.

Opening the front door, stood before me were the two constables I had met the morning I had found Bill Longman.

'Mr Nicolson' said the older one, 'had a complaint about you.' He shone a torch in my face. 'Where did you get the shiner, looks like there might be something in the complaint after all?'

'Yes, had a punch up with three of your local yobs.'

'Three was it, could you get dressed Mr Nicolson and come along with us to the station?'

'What are you arresting me?'

'No you are helping with our inquiries, of course if you refuse then. Better to come along nice and peaceful looks better that way.'

'OK, OK, I'll come peacefully, come in while I get dressed. At least you will have to feed me breakfast; the larder here is getting a bit bare.'

'Surely Mr Nicolson' said the younger constable 'mind you, you must have a strong stomach if you fancy a police breakfast.'

Twenty-Four

Liskeard Police Station had not changed overmuch from my last visit. However my hosts on this occasion, at four a.m. felt it better I should be introduced to one of their first class cells, and locked me up no doubt to stop me doing a runner. Although as they were quick to point out I had not been arrested, merely helping with enquires.

Funny, only with a blanket and a dirty looking mattress over a metal bed with weak springs, it all seemed to be getting familiar, far too familiar, but I did drop off easily into a deep sleep of the innocent.

At nine in the morning, light flooding the cell, I was woken with a cup of tea, which was just as revolting as I remembered. I used the en-suite facilities which were not top notch being a bucket in the corner. Soon breakfast turned up, I ate a little but the young constable had been right it was only slightly better than the tea.

The decor was all grey gloss paint on the walls with a black floor. A high window on the end wall cast light into the cell. A heavy door with a spy hole was closed and I guessed locked. And so I waited.

In about an hour I was taken to an interview room, where Inspector Montague was sitting at a table. He looked only slightly better than I felt. The air was thick from his pipe smoke.

'Morning Nicolson' he said.

No 'Mr' I noted and he sounded irritated, had I upset his Sunday morning routine? 'Inspector, I won't say it's good to see you. Found out who killed Bill Longman yet?' I said sitting down opposite him. 'Do you think we can have a window open, it's like a fog in here?'

Montague motioned to the constable, who had brought me from the cell and remained, to open the window.

'Don't worry inspector I'm not going to try and dive through it to escape.'

'No I'm sure you will not. As to Mr Longman I cannot say we have made much progress in the case not a lot to go on, as yet.'

'Have you turned anything up Mr Nicolson, because you seem to have stirred up a hornets' nest?'

I wondered how much Montague knew. So I just played dumb. 'Can't say I'm aware of that, other than perhaps, getting up the nose of the Allan-Cleary's.'

'Yes and what do you know about them, and why should you go out of your way to annoy them?'

'Nothing much other than my Aunt knew the old man, from the war I believe, why have they complained? Have I annoyed them?'

Montague shook his head. 'No Mr Nicolson the only complaint we have is from a Mr Coath last night who says you assaulted him.'

'That's right inspector, I take it one was him along with two others.'

'Oh we know all about Coath, what you might call one of the local yobs. In fact if that had been the only complaint we would have left it until this morning. No need for the dramatic call in the middle of the night dragging you from your bed.'

'So why was I a guest of your hostelry last night?'

'Why indeed Mr Nicolson, it appears for some reason you have ruffled the feathers of MI5, they asked us to bring you in. Know anything about that? Does it have any bearing on the death of Longman?'

'No idea' I lied, I was now certain it was them who had taken me, kidnapped me, but why? I tried a bit of fishing and told Montague about my attempted visit to Gweebarra.

It was obvious Montague did not believe me, but he said there had been no complaint from the Allan-Cleary's. But then how did he know I had been annoying the Allan-Clarey's unless through local gossip. But he struck me as a good copper with his ear to the ground.

'There is a Major Lanyon on his way to interview you. Coming from London as far as I can tell, these secret fellows never give much away. Always seem full of their own importance to me, as if nothing else matters but the security of the realm. Law and order means nothing to them.' He stared at me, picking up his pipe aimlessly, and then thinking better of it he put it down.

'Not all that happy with these types on my patch, they usually mean trouble that we have to clear up', he raised an inquiring eyebrow.

'Sorry Inspector I'm in the dark as much as you, probably more so, I think we will just have to wait for Major....' I searched for his name.

'Lanyon, Mr Nicolson, Major Lanyon.'

Twenty-five

Major Lanyon wore a Coldstream Guards tie, he was younger than I had expected, in his early forties. He had a neat blonde moustache and close cropped blonde hair; his eyes were dark brown almost black. His turn out, a blue pinstriped suit, was smart, that, given his background, might be expected. If that was his real background, you could never tell with these people. Although I was well aware a lot of service officers did find their way into the SIS, I had come across a few in Northern Ireland. On internal security duties.

'Ah Nicolson' he said when he was shown in, not offering a hand to shake. 'Thank you Inspector, the constable can leave as well' he said to Montague dismissing him like a flunky, which I could tell was not at all to his liking.

As they left, Lanyon placed his briefcase on the table; he undid his suit coat, vaguely brushed off his chair with his hand and sat down.

'So' he grinned 'you have led us a pretty chase Nicolson.'

'Had I known you, whoever you are, were after me I might have been more amenable sir?' *Why did I call him sir? I was no longer in the service, must be habit,* I thought, and smiled at him.

'Quite so, the local lads did not handle it well. Should have done better.' He opened his briefcase and took out a thin brown file; opening it he studied an equally thin sheaf of papers.

I tried to read it upside down but it was too far away.

'Robin Nicolson, you left the Royal Marines, what, eighteen months ago, having served in Cyprus, Northern Ireland three tours, and the Falklands War, left a marine after nine years, conduct excellent.' He looked up at me.

'Sounds like me might be hundreds of others 'I said making a conscious effort not to say sir.

'And your late Aunt, Miss Carolyn Thompson, made you her sole beneficiary which is why you are down here in Cornwall?'

'That's it Major, got it in one.'

'No other reason Nicolson?'

'None.'

He took a large manila envelope out of his briefcase, and removed from it three exercise books, my aunt's diaries.

'Now I wondered where they had gone.'

Lanyon rested his hands on them. 'You know what's in these Nicolson?'

'Most of it, although I had not got around to reading the third one.'

He pushed them across the table to me. 'I think you should finish reading them, I'll see if I can rustle up some tea.'

'I warn you Major it's made with condensed milk in this place, awful stuff, not a good establishment by any stretch of the imagination, never going to get five stars.'

'Thanks for the warning I will see what I can do' he said, leaving the room.

I opened the third journal, it read;

'London Monday January 10th 1949.

This is a surprise; I find I have to restart my secret diary, I thought it was all over. When Allan-Cleary and his group were arrested, I thought it was an end.

That was in summer of 1943, not long after the invasion of Sicily, now six years on, a telegram arrived from dear Bill Longman, I could not believe it, and all it said was.

'He's back at Gweebarra.

Bill.'

I thought he would have been executed, or still in prison, I had not checked, I did not want to know, I trusted my Government. Now he was out, free.

I had left Naval Intelligence in 1943; having turned down Ian Fleming's offer, Admiral Godfrey sent me a personal letter of thanks.

But I continued working at Western Approaches Plymouth as a translator, doing my bit, until the end of the war when it was all over.

In 1945, I moved to London, Liz was demobbed we took a flat together, we needed each other then. Dear Dad had left us both reasonably well off, what people call comfortable. I began pursuing a writing career with freelance newspaper articles, the odd short story.

I had not told Liz about what happened, I had signed the official secrets act. As far as she knew Dad had died in an accident on Cyprus better it stayed that way for her. So I merely told her I was going down to Cornwall to see an old friend.

Thursday January 20th 1949.

Took the train to Plymouth today, the city resembles a huge building site rebuilding after the Blitz, changed there to a Liskeard train and got off at St.Germans. Bill met me there with a Morris Van.

'You look fine Carolyn' he greeted me taking my case 'wish we were meeting under better circumstances.' That was unlikely I knew I was reasonably pretty or thought so, but he did not seem interested in me in that way.

I told him I had been in touch with NI but Admiral Godfrey had retired and Ian was back in Civvy Street. Only Ted Merrett, the ever faithful civil servant was still there, he was good enough to see me. I told him what I knew, he said.

'Carolyn, I cannot talk about the case. But you know our work is never, was never, black and white. A deal was done, probably for information, and still is come to that. I know it is of no consolation to you, it is not justice for your father'.

'And many others Ted' I pointed out.

'Quite so, but there is nothing to be done'.

That was about it, what the deal was he did not reveal, perhaps he did not even know.

I told Bill we had both signed the official secrets act, we could not just blow the whistle on him, if we did that we would end up in the Tower, not Allan-Cleary

It was then, or in the next few days I decided to move to Downderry. I had been staying at the Inn-on-the-Shore and noticed some bungalows being built at Beach Road, overlooking the sea; I saw the builder and bought one, having the design altered to my own requirements. He thought I was mad but did as I asked. I suppose I was trying to recreate the bungalow at Kantara in Cyprus. It was all a bit on impulse really.

Wednesday 16th March 1949.

It was difficult to convince Liz why I wanted to move to Cornwall. She considered I was burying myself in a wild remote land, and could not see the reason. And of course would miss me.

I told her that to me it was like Cyprus, to a degree this was true, a slower way of life, the county was almost an island, with an ancient mystic history.

Friday 24th June 1949.

Well here I am but what am I to do about Allan-Cleary on my own, he is still at Gweebarra, as far as I can tell he does not go back to Ireland often. Bill is not much help he just wants to shoot him and I am sure would if I did not restrain him.

Saturday 24th December 1949.

It's Christmas Eve, my first Christmas in my own home Kantara, although it does not feel much like home, not like Cyprus at all.

There might be a way forward by taking a civil case against Allan-Cleary. I must find some misdemeanour that I can get him into court with and then humiliate him.

Tuesday 3rd October 1950.

A new decade, my investigations of the Allan-Cleary's have largely drawn a blank. There must be some way to get at them. Yet they seem to do nothing and have no flaws. But an idea I did have, but do I have the nerve? It is said the pen is mightier than the sword.

Wednesday 17 January 1951.

After a lot of soul searching I have done a terrible thing, from frustration, I have sent RP Allan-Cleary a poison pen letter. To let him know he will not get away with it. Posted in London made up of pasted newspaper cuttings no writing not even on the address, so melodramatic I need to get away.

Thursday 24 April 1952 Cyprus.

I have been close to giving up or telling Bill to shoot RP. I have sent no more letters. I have returned to Cyprus for three months and have opened up the bungalow at Kantara it has been empty for ten years.

It is wonderful here in the spring; the wild flowers are a riot of colour, so warm and dry after the cold wet Cornish winter. I thought it might feel like coming home but it has not worked. I did consider returning here permanently but as much as I love the island I don't think so. Too many memories here.

However, get to the point Carolyn, I was in Nicosia doing some shopping and passed the main police station. It was on the spur of the moment. I went inside and asked the desk sergeant if Inspector Kemal Faiz was there. He smiled broadly and said there was no inspector there of that name, however they did have a Chief Inspector of that name.

Kemal was little changed, only a touch of grey at his temples and the beginnings of crow's feet at the corners of his eyes, those dark brown eyes always with a touch of humour about them. Like many Turks he had that inscrutable air about him you were never quite sure what he was thinking. However I knew Kemal to be utterly trustworthy. His eyes lit up when I was shown into his office.

'Miss Carolyn Thompson, how lovely to see you after all these years' he beamed. Coming from behind his desk to shake my hand and help me to a seat. Back in his seat he continued. 'I presume it is Miss?' he said raising an eyebrow. Although I was sure he had immediately noticed no ring. But with such manners he would never say so.

'I'm afraid so Chief Inspector' I noticed the row of medal ribbons on his chest, I'm no expert but one looked like the DSC. 'So you did not stay in Cyprus during the war' I said, indicating the medal ribbons.

'No I joined the Navy, served in the home waters briefly, and then Naval Intelligence got hold of me, I was with them for a spell.'

My mouth must have dropped open.

'You are surprised Carolyn?'

'Yes Kemal, you see I served in NI as well.'

I was as surprised by that revelation as much as my Aunt had been thirty years earlier. Major Lanyon returned, with cups on a tray, and some custard cream biscuits on a plate.

'Fresh milk Nicolson.'

'I'm impressed Major, I suppose rank has its privileges.'

He smiled. 'Please continue' he said indicating the diary.

I drank my tea, soaking a couple of custard creams, which made Lanyon wrinkle his nose in obvious distaste. I returned to my reading.

'Come' said Kemal getting up reaching for his peaked cap. 'We will have some tea in more relaxed surroundings'; that I learnt was his answer to everything.

He told the sergeant where he could be found and we walked outside to a cafe on Lendra Street where obviously Kemal was well known, it was well shaded by one of the city's walls, great bastions, a tribute to the Crusaders building skills, and only a few minutes from the station.

There, he was right, we could talk more freely I told him what had happened to me, everything but writing the poison pen letter; I was too ashamed of that to own up.

'And now you feel robbed of justice, an elusive principal Carolyn. 'Injustice swift, erect and unconfin'd, sweeps the wide earth, and tramples o'er mankind.'

'Who said that Kemal?'

'Our friend Homer.'

'A Greek Kemal?'

'Indeed as you say a Greek, but an ancient Greek.'

'Does he have anything to say on revenge?' I asked.

Kemal thought for a moment. 'Francis Bacon called revenge "a kind of wild justice."

I could not get that out of my mind for days a "wild justice" was consuming me, bathing me in its glow.

Tuesday 15th July 1952.

I will be going home shortly, to Cornwall, well that is something resolved. Cornwall is home now, I am bound to it, I realise because of RP, until I obtain revenge or justice.

Cyprus is so hot now. Although up at Kantara it is cool I shall keep the bungalow there, if I can resolve my quest, put the ghosts to rest, then I might return, I want to. I really do this was home for so long.

During my visit I have seen Kemal many times, and spent much time with him and his family at his home in Famagusta near the sea. He is married to an English woman, Marion quite beautiful, with a nature to match, she was a wren, they met during the war, and I have learnt Kemal's own mother was English. He has two small boys; they look so much like him.

Kemal has told me most of his time with NI was spent in the Mediterranean during the war, he did meet Ian Fleming briefly in London. But never came across RP outside of Cyprus in that time.

However Kemal unknowingly sparked something one evening, we were enjoying the sea breeze on the veranda. Marion had just put the boys to bed.

We did not often talk of RP, it lay between us, I guessed he knew it was playing on my mind, but that night he said he felt, 'Allan-Cleary is locked in his own living prison you know Carolyn, he cannot escape, he must always be looking over his shoulder'. I know he was trying to help me, to put me at ease.

I blurted out how we had caught Allan-Cleary at Gweebarra, and my part in it I knew I should not.

'My goodness how exciting for you' said Kemal.

I told him Commander Frank Slocum was put out that we did not catch White Fang. But I did not believe he existed I felt intelligence fellows sometimes got carried away in their own world imagining agents everywhere.

'Oh no Carolyn' said Kemal 'White Fang existed, or as a code word for an Abwehr agent it was used certainly. I came across it in 1942 in Cairo and the Western Desert. Some believed it referred to a code book,

Jack London's White Fang; the German's used books, novels in that way. But no I'm sure I saw him once, he existed.'

The inscrutable smile crossed his face and he would say no more as there was nothing else he could say about it. Somehow I doubted that but Kemal was no gossip not like me, taking the official secrets seriously. But he was a dear friend to me.

'Always looking over his shoulder' Kemal had said. Could I lock him tighter into that prison?

That started a chain of thought in me. Before I left for home I had resolved to blackmail RP. If I was ever found out, if it ever came to court it would all come out. It could not fail. I would make his life a living death, a misery, a constant worry. Before long he would wish he had been executed.'

I put the diary down.

'Have you read this Major?' I said, Lanyon was standing by the window.

Turning he said 'Yes Nicolson all of them, quite revealing, your aunt was extraordinary.'

'Did she do it? Did she blackmail Allan-Cleary?'

'Yes took him for thousands a six figure sum over the years. All in cash I think or the equivalent.'

'Well they must have killed her and Bill Longman. Not RP obviously he's too old, although he would have egged on that son of his, Martin, to do it.'

'You think so Nicolson? I somehow doubt it, I'm not even sure they found out it was your Aunt, until you began stumbling about causing a fuss Nicolson. She covered her tracks too well. When RP was younger he might have murdered your aunt but not now, there was little point.'

'Unless the money was running out Major?'

'No, that was not the case, he did pay thousands for years of the family's money came near to bankruptcy, but HM Government has been paying it for the last five.'

I laughed out loud at that. 'You're telling me, Major, my grey haired Aunt was blackmailing MI5, and you were paying her?'

'Something like that and happy to do it' he smiled his black eyes sparkling reflecting the neon light; I had the feeling he was in his element.

'Although it was the taxpayers' Lanyon continued 'some contingency found in White Hall. Your Aunt was clever, we never rumbled her. She used a numbered Swiss Bank account. Impossible to trace after the Nome's of Zurich had it in their vaults.

Then according to her diaries she sent it directly to charities. In all sorts of strange places, going directly to charities anonymously of course, the only common one over the last few years was a PO Box in Northern Cyprus; it came up a few times over the years. We should have had someone look at that, it should have rung bells, but with Northern Cyprus under the Turks now there's not much point, hard to find anything there so not a high priority.'

'So why are you guarding Allan-Cleary, surely not from my Aunt, Major?'

'No certainly not, that was just an irritant. Perhaps if I tell you Nicolson it will end now for your family and you will drop it.'

Lanyon sighed gathering his thoughts. 'When we caught Allan-Cleary in 1943, it did not take him long to betray his Nazi masters. We rounded up dozens of agents on his information. Mind you that on its own did not save him from the gallows; he was still down for execution.'

'A last cigarette and a firing squad nice and clean eh Major?'

'No you have been watching too many films. They hang traitors in this country. Even now the death penalty continues to remain in force for a handful of crimes, most notably that of treason Nicolson' he said raising his eyebrows.

'They still have a fully operational gallows ready to use, in Wandsworth Prison I believe.'

'What's that, a warning Major?'

"Certainly not, just a matter of interest".

'Did you get White Fang, whoever he was?'

'No, we think he got away via Southern Ireland, and it was Allan-Cleary's connection with the IRA kept him alive. His willingness eventually to betray them as well as the Nazi's was why we did a deal, and agreed to protect him for life; he remained an active source, so his past had to remain secret, as if he had never been caught.

Recently we got a sniff, one of the splinter groups of the IRA had found him out, realised he had betrayed them as well as the Abwehr Agents, now they are out to kill him.'

'What after all these years Major, you're joking?'

'Joking, not about the Provisional IRA, they have long memories, especially with people who betray them. You should know that having served in Ireland.'

'I was on the streets, not with intelligence Major. I still find it hard to believe they would be after an old man.' I thought about that briefly. 'Yes Major you're right they would go after him.'

'Your Aunt was willing to keep the punishment she meted out to the Allan-Cleary's going after all these years Nicolson. In my experience grudges don't go away.'

He had me there, such people were consumed by an ideal, be it revenge or a cause, and I would never have put my Aunt in that category. Or was I in it now carrying on the vendetta for my Grandfather and the others?

'What about my Aunt, Major, who murdered her?'

'No murder Nicolson, natural causes, I have looked into it the local police here are convinced as well.'

'And Bill Longman, did he fall on his own knife, backwards?'

The Major smiled at that. 'Longman was we think involved in the local underworld so I'm informed. Inspector Montague will get to the bottom of it I'm sure.'

I was far from convinced by the Major's dismissal of two potential murders, but said nothing.

Lanyon got up. 'I'll see Montague about your release Nicolson, carry on, and finish the diary.'

Twenty-six

I returned to the diary which now consisted mainly of monthly payment details, where it was paid and how much. It started with five hundred pounds in November 1952. There was little else now other than the odd comment like.

'Tuesday 2 June 1953.
Elizabeth II crowned today.
Saturday 18 December 1954.
Rioting in Cyprus by Greeks demanding "Enosis" Union with Greece, it will never happen, don't they know this, that poor island, and how will this effect Kemal and Marion?
Monday 28 November 1955.
State of alert in Cyprus, two more British soldiers killed. They have a good man out there now as Governor Sir John Harding, can he control the meddling priests and steer his way through the labyrinth.
Wednesday 31 October 1956.
Is the world going to end? There are risings in Hungary, Soviet tanks on the streets. And we have invaded Egypt, what are we doing, do they think we are still an imperial power? And poor Cyprus continues to bleed from its self inflicted wounds.
Thursday 2 October 1958.
The worst news today from Kemal, he and his family have had enough and are leaving Cyprus, his home, for good. Oh! It is so sad. I have cried for my friends.
Kemal has resigned from the Cyprus Police and is immigrating to Australia. I don't suppose I shall ever see him again. Should I sell the bungalow at Kantara? No I don't think I could it would completely sever my link to Dad and, in a way, to Joe.'

By 1960 the monthly payment had risen to one thousand pounds a month, that payment going to a PO Box in *'Fredricksburg, Virginia, USA'*.

I began to wonder how my aunt managed to trace that the payment had been made and arrived at its destination in a world before computers. There must have been some receipt system, but I had found no evidence of it no paperwork whatsoever. Certainly from what I knew of my aunt, and what I had found so far, she had not profited directly from her blackmail activities.

Another entry caught my eye.

'Saturday 24 January 1959.

Mike Hawthorne, the golden boy of motor racing, was killed two days ago, only twenty-nine, killed driving his own sports car, in a crash on the Guildford by-pass near his home in Surrey. He reminded me so much of dear Joe, my golden boy, he was about the same age.

"They shall not grow old as we that are left grow old.

Age shall not weary them...."

It still haunts so much to think of him does the pain ever go.'

One thing I noticed about all the diaries, and especially the third one, there was no mention about the family other than the odd reference to my Grandmother Liz, and her father, my great granddad. Nothing about the rest of us, it was as if we were in a completely different compartment of her life. Kept strictly separate and apart.

'Monday 17 December 1973.

The country is going down the pan, as Bill puts it, industry now on a three day week.'

Payment that month went to *'Milan, Italy, of two thousand five hundred'*.

Flicking on I came across.

118

'Saturday 20 July 1974.

The Turks have invaded Cyprus because of the Greek coup against President Makarios. Where will it end? What of the bungalow? Thankfully it is off the beaten track.'

I remembered that summer well. My unit going to reinforce the island garrison, the feeling of apprehension we might get sucked into a proper shooting war. But it had not happened; the UN had intervened and created the "green line" dividing the island between the Turkish north and Greek Cypriot south. I served with the UN for several months, when I got to know the island well. That month the Allan-Cleary's had coughed up two thousand five hundred pounds to a PO Box in Canada for an orphanage. My Aunt must have done quite a bit of home work on charities.

The last entry was a payment in March 1984 only a few weeks ago, four thousand pounds to Munich in West Germany.

So my aunt had milked the Allan-Cleary's for over thirty years, for something over three hundred thousand pounds. I had to admire her, how she had kept it going so long, even after the Government began picking up the tab. Although she did not know that, which convinced me she had been murdered, because they had finally discovered who she was. Perhaps she had even told them she was about to blow the whistle on them. For her final aim was still to expose RP for what he was and what he had done. And how much longer would RP live. She was an old lady too, what could authority do to her. I was her insurance that much was clear now.

Twenty-Seven

Major Lanyon returned looking uncomfortable, and his cheeks were flushed crimson. He went over to the window seemingly to examine the vista of Liskeard on a dull spring day.

'Finished your aunt's diaries Nicolson?' he said without turning.

'Just about' I said 'she appears to have fleeced the Allan-Cleary's for a sizeable sum Major.'

'Indeed she did, a very clever lady.' He turned from the window and came back to the table sitting across the table from me. 'It appears that Inspector Montague is not all that happy to release you and would rather have you up before the local magistrates.'

'What for? Causing an affray or does he think I'm going to bump off the people at Gweebarra. Or maybe I'm still in the frame for Bill Longman's murder. But then he told me I was not, so it's a no to both questions. Might it be that he really does not trust you lot, or thinks I'm tied up with you?'

'You could be right Nicolson. But the good Inspector wants you released, if released you are, into someone's care so as you don't run amuck.'

'What bail or something? Surely the great MI5 can tell a local plod where to get off?'

'Yes we could but we don't like stepping on local corns or using bully boy tactics. Perhaps there is someone you might stay with like your parents, perhaps?'

Well that was a non-starter; and it would mean returning home, I would rather have gone back to cells than that. Or was it they wanted me well out of the way, not sniffing around or anything. 'I don't think that's a good idea Major, my mother might cause more trouble than me.'

'Nobody else?'

'What about the doctor Eve Reilly, she was my aunt's doctor.' I do not know why I said that. Other than I wanted to see her again, and stay in the area, not go back to London, but then I hardly knew Eve, she might well refuse.

'Ah, the lady with the red sports car Nicolson, a doctor a responsible person, could be ideal, I'll see what Montague says.'

He got up, but turned at the door. 'I assume she will agree?'

'I don't know for certain Major. I'm just hoping she will, because I can't stand much more of the condensed milk or cold beans in this establishment.'

It was an hour later Lanyon returned this time with Montague. 'The Inspector here is happy that you stay with Doctor Reilly' said the Major.

'That's right' said Montague. 'However I want you to sign in here every seventy two hours, until this business is cleared up Mr Nicolson', empty pipe in hand he used the stem to emphasise here being the police station.

'Any further forward in your investigations into the Bill Longman murder Inspector?'

'Steady progress Mr Nicolson. Now I have had a chat with Doctor Reilly, she knows the score. Nice lady, you have landed on your feet there I hope you appreciate it. So just behave yourself. No more punch-up's.'

He sounded more like my father and there was an air of envy from the Inspector. So Eve with her gregarious nature had won him over. Good for her and good for me I thought.

'Nicolson' said Lanyon extending his hand, 'I doubt we will meet again. You can keep the diaries, but remember you have signed the official secrets act. Just because you are in civvy Street now it still applies. Any attempt to publish will have you in extremely hot water.'

I shook his hand. "I'll bear that in mind Major, especially as you still hang traitors for treason". With that Lanyon picked up his briefcase nodded to Montague and left.

'Doctor Reilly is on her way to pick you up. Nothing you want to tell me now we are on our own?'

'Not a thing Inspector, I will try and be a good boy. But I would point out trouble has come looking for me in all this.'

'Here' he said handing me another of his cards 'you can get me day or night Mr Nicolson, day or night remember that.' Montague was persistent I had to give him that.

Twenty-Eight

An hour later I was sat in the passenger seat of Eve's red Triumph Spitfire. She looked curiously different wearing a base ball cap, emblazoned with the *'Toronto Maple Leafs',* which hid her eyes. Thankfully in the car she removed the hat tossing it into the space behind us. Her blonde hair was shining.

'That's better Eve I can see your face now, who are the Toronto Maple Leafs then?'

'Ice hockey team back home.'

'I keep having to thank you Eve, you are making a habit of bailing me out' I said when we had set off.

'Well it was hardly that, if it had involved hard cash I might have thought twice. Although I admit I don't think I have ever signed for a man before and life with you I have to say is exciting' she said giggling.

I liked the thought she would think twice if money was involved not just leave me lingering with the cops.

Eve took the road toward Downderry to pick up my gear. The day was still grey and the hood was up on the Triumph, which gave us a space of enclosed intimacy. She had told me she was having a few days off and was going to stay on the north coast in a caravan away from phones and hospitals and sick people, so I was going to have to tag along with her for her to perform her duty. A prospect that I had to admit had a certain appeal.

'Can't remember the last time I had a beach holiday, I'm already looking forward to it' was my reply.

Eve glanced sideways at me; those penetrating grey eyes had a curious look, as if testing me. I had to glance away.

There was something about this woman that was strangely compelling. Was this the beginning of something special I thought, I did not want to use the word love?

After collecting a few things for me from Kantara we went back to Minions to pick up Eve's weekend bag. We stocked up with a few essential provisions from the village shop and then headed for the north Cornish coast.

Across the wide grey green bleak expanses of Bodmin Moor travelling through showers of mizzling rain the going was slow until we reached the A30 trunk road, which cut a swathe across the moor. At Bodmin we turned toward Wadebridge following the Camel River. The weather improved in that the rain stopped but it remained dull with heavy looking clouds threatening more rain. The coast here was barren compared to the gentle wooded south coast; here all was exposed to the Atlantic gales.

It was late afternoon by the time we reached St.Mawgan, and ran on right down to the sea at Mawgan Porth, a horseshoe bay with a wide expanse of white sand. A few bungalows lined the hills behind the bay and a handful of shops and hostelries were closer to the sands.

Eve found the small caravan park with only half a dozen vans easily for she had been there before; it was shielded from the beach and weather by low sand dunes dotted with green coarse grasses and reeds.

The key to the caravan was under a plant pot and Eve let us into what would be home for a few days. We unloaded the car which took all of five minutes. Made up the beds, the bed for Eve a sofa bed for me which was narrow and looked none too comfortable, the van was small and could sleep four at a pinch in basically two rooms living and sleeping.

A walk even in the dull chilly weather was a good idea from Eve who told me she liked wild remote places. Well this was wild and remote.

The tide was far out, the sea leaving a dark blue line between the two ends of the horseshoe marked clearly by the cliffs of the two headlands. We could see the foam of the sea crashing against the rocks but did not venture very close, just stood still looking at the sea's power.

'I have seen some striking sunsets here Rob, almost painful in their beauty' said Eve.

We were both wrapped up in anoraks against the cold and damp.

'Don't think you will get much of one today' I said adding, 'been here often then Eve?'

'Yes a few times Rob, helps me unwind' she looked at her watch. 'An hour or so and the Merryman Inn will be open, because I'm not cooking for you buster' she said smiling broadly at me.

'No need I'll pay, but what about breakfast, we did not buy all that bacon and eggs for appearances I take it?'

'As they say tomorrow is another day Rob' with that she took my arm getting closer and we walked on across the wide expanse of sand.

It was near dark by the time we reached the Merryman Inn which was open for business. Two other customers had got there before us. Even that was surprising I thought given the weather and the early season. It had felt as if we were the only two people on earth.

I got us some drinks and menus from the bar; the fare was plain and simple if a little limited. After ordering our meal we sat silently for a while.

Eve broke the silence asking. 'Have you a favourite restaurant Rob?'

'Favourite' I thought a little 'there was a place on Cyprus 'The Bunch of Grapes' wonderful Cypriot dishes beef stifado, kleftiko, cooked in clay ovens, best chips I have tasted, eating under the stars, don't know if it's still there now, what about you Eve?'

'The Bunch of Grapes sounds wonderful. My favourite is on Pier 39 in San Francisco' she shyly smiled. 'Great sea food and clam chowder melts in your mouth.'

I looked into those inquiring grey blue eyes that were sparkling now with highlights from the open fire's flames reflected in them; it had a curious effect I had to drag my gaze away from them.

'What do you intend to do now Rob about your Aunt and the legacy?'

'I don't really know Eve; I feel I should do something for my aunt, after all she asked me to, but what? Why don't you read the diaries, give me your opinion?'

'OK Rob I'd be happy to.'

With that the food arrived, we both had the same, it was good, described as *"fisherman's pie"*. We exchanged little chat, I began to wonder if this was really such a good idea but I had little choice.

We were back at the caravan before ten and soon in our separate beds; Eve took the diaries to her bed and began reading by torch light. I thought sleep might be difficult but I went out like a light perhaps it was the bracing Atlantic sea air and here I could relax. Here I did not have to do anything, for my dead Aunt or my baying relatives, they could all wait.

Twenty-Nine

'Come on rise and shine, last one in the water makes breakfast' said Eve pretty close to my ear. Then she was shaking me awake.

Opening my eyes I was momentarily blinded by sunlight flooding the caravan. Eve was dressed in a dark single piece swimsuit that was tight to her body. She looked fresh and alluring. She had to be joking was my first thought. But the look on her face told me otherwise.

'Be right with you' I said, and tried to turn over, but Eve swept the bed clothes off me and I groaned.

'Come on big boy, I'm on my way,' with that she was gone.

I climbed stiffly from the sofa bed which had done none of my joints any favours. Swimming trunks I did not have but a pair of shorts served just as well.

Outside, the day was in total contrast to the previous day. The sky was a deep bright blue with no sign of clouds. The sunlight even that early in the morning was bouncing back off the sand promising a hot day.

Eve I could see had reached the water's edge. 'Looks like your cooking breakfast old boy' I said out loud. Taking a few deep breaths to get the lungs working I set off after Eve at a gentle jog.

The water was freezing when I reached it and ventured in.

'Come on get a move on' cried Eve, the water up to her breasts where she stood waving, 'it's great.'

Liar, I thought, she was worse than a sergeant major.

Seeing my obvious hesitation Eve cried. 'Thought you were a big tough commando' and then she plunged under the water.

Was there a mocking edge to her words? Or was it just her humour, after all the Canadians liked to rib the Brits I told myself. I knew there was no way of escaping my fate. So I ran at the water,

127

and when it reached my middle, dived in. Hoping this vigorous assault might make the Atlantic water warmer. It did not; it was freezing cold enough to take your breath away. The water after all was bound to be cold, it had come from Eve's home, Canada, and that was frozen stiff six months of the year. No wonder she was used to it.

It was not long and we were back at the caravan park, having washed the salt water off at the outside cold shower. Bacon and eggs were frying on the small gas stove. We had both dressed and had that glow of warmth after being so cold. I had to admit it was a bracing way to start the day. Providing it did not bring on a heart attack or pneumonia.

'So Rob, what shall we do on this beautiful day?'

Moving bacon around the pan I called over my shoulder. 'Up to you Eve, after all you're the jailer.'

'I'll never be that Rob' she said seriously. 'I got through most of your aunt's diaries last night.'

'You must have been up late, what did you think, is she nuts?'

'I was up late, they were fascinating, and she was far from nuts, a pity...' her voice trailed off with regret.

'A pity about what?'

'A pity I did not know her better Rob. One thing I came across I think I had heard about before. That plane Allan-Cleary or White Fang or somebody sabotaged took off near here at the RAF base.'

'How do you know that?' I asked, bringing her breakfast to the small table in the sleeping area, which was now converted to a living space via the sofa bed reverting to its first role.

'I've a bit of a thing for looking around cemeteries; I find it fascinating; I came across a couple of graves at St.Columb Minor. RAF pilots from a plane went down in 1943; I think it might be the same plane your aunt talks about. Apparently local talk has it there might have been gold on board, sovereigns that sort of thing.'

'Buried treasure, should we get some diving suits' I suggested.

'After your display this morning I don't think that's a good idea' she said grinning.

Within an hour we stood in front of two gravestones at the Fairpark Cemetery at St.Columb Minor. It was a scene of tranquillity. The grass was lush and green wild spring flowers carpeted the ground. The only sound the hum of bees.

'It took them some time to identify these men. At first they were thought to be seamen' said Eve. 'Apparently' she continued in a low voice, although there was no sign of anybody else, 'some other bodies from the plane are buried in Newquay, again unknown. But as we know now, some passengers on the flight were on a secret mission, their identity never revealed.'

'Known only unto God' I said.

'That's right' said Eve.

The two headstones were marked with RAF eagles, moss had begun to grow in the letters of the motto, and I rubbed them clean. "Per Ardua ad Astra" I said.

'Sorry my Latin's none to good' said Eve.

'Through Struggles to the Stars, motto of the RAF.'

Eve nodded, 'yes of course.'

One headstone was for a flight lieutenant the other a flight sergeant, the sergeant from the Royal Australian Air Force.

'He was a long way from home' I said, pointing at the sergeant's headstone.

'Another casualty of Allan-Cleary's war' said Eve.

'Casualty, no he was a victim, came half way around the world to end like that, a victim of that traitor. Are you sure about this Eve?'

'I talked to an old boy a few months ago; he was in the Home Guard at the time, reserved occupation. He saw the plane blow up in mid air shortly after takeoff. The plane was a Warwick, a passenger version of the Wellington Bomber, had twenty people on board when it took off from St.Mawgan.'

'Twenty people' I said in disbelief.

'The Court of Inquiry said the crash was due to fog or engine failure or trying to avoid another aircraft. The Home Guard man never believed that, he was never called as a witness, although he only learnt about the inquiry much later. We of course know what was going on and how callous your government was.'

I stared at Eve for a moment, the grey eyes were cold, no emotion in them. But she was right the government was callous but governments can be, sometimes have to be, but governments are not people. Not individuals. She must have looked into the plane crash but then people got interested in all sorts of things.

'No Eve, responsibility lies with Allan-Cleary the callous part of the government is that he never danced at the end of a rope.'

'Yes that too Rob. But your Aunt certainly made him pay.'

She took my hand then, as we stood there, and squeezed it.

'Your Aunt has passed her torch onto you Rob. What are you going to do? You cannot ignore a death wish. You have to act.'

Eve's eyes still showed nothing, not a flicker of emotion; her statement was just a fact of my legacy, although she sounded almost happy about it. She was right of course but I did not answer for I had none, there was nothing to say. I found it strange she made the sign of the cross, I did not equate her with being religious, but then I knew little about her. We walked away back to the car together, hand in hand. Things were going well with this beautiful woman I thought.

Thirty

The rest of the day we spent wandering around the small Cornish coastal towns of Penzance and St.Ives with their cohorts of tourists. We visited art galleries in the latter and had lunch in the former. Eve and I did not talk much. By mid afternoon we had returned to the caravan at Mawgan Porth.

Eve changed into her swimsuit but we lay outside the caravan on towels on the grass and listened to the radio. There was a report of growing tension around Orgreave Coking Plant in South Yorkshire. The Miners Strike was now in its tenth week the announcer said.

'So the war intensifies' said Eve. 'Your Government lured Scargill and the miners into a war they are doomed to lose. Clever, very clever.'

I thought she had been asleep lying there with her eyes closed. The rise and fall of her chest had been fascinating me. Did she know I had been watching her? Somehow I thought so.

'I think you exaggerate with the civil war comparison Eve. Look at us here enjoying ourselves.'

"People enjoy themselves in wars; in fact emotions are often heightened. There are quiet times; it's not always blood and guts. Even your aunt enjoyed some of her war in some way I expect, she had a thing about Bill, don't know it was reciprocated. Thought anything more about her legacy Rob? The debt of honour.' She turned over raising herself up on her elbows to look down at me.

'Yes I need to confront them. I know that. I need to come face to face with RP Allan-Cleary, his son will not do. But how and why are MI5 protecting him? From who? Did they expect my Aunt to go up there and kill him? Or was it Bill Longman?

Did they kill my Aunt and Bill? They had blackmailed the Allan-Cleary's for years, why do they need protection now? Someone who betrayed his Nazi masters, I'm missing something in all this...'

'Rob, you being an ex-commando with all those skills should be able to get passed a couple of goons in suits.'

'Perhaps' I said vaguely, the seeds of an idea growing in my mind.

'I'm going for a swim Rob' said Eve getting to her feet.

'OK' I said 'I'll stay here and think for a while, be careful.' She walked away, her buttocks swaying provocatively under the thin swimsuit, but I had other things on my mind, dragged my eyes away from her, gazing up at the clear sky.

Eve shook me awake with her foot. She had showered and was wrapped in a towel, her wet hair plastered to her head. She stood blocking out the sun that was descending toward the western horizon. The sun light glistened off her wet blond hair; almost halo like, it was a startling effect.

'Hey big boy don't sleep in the sun you'll burn.'

Eve had been gone barely an hour, I had lasted ten minutes before falling asleep.

'Come inside, I have something to show you' she said smiling.

Inside the caravan she closed the curtains over the small windows, then turned toward me and dropped the towel to the floor stepping toward me. Then she was in my arms naked I could hardly believe it.

What remained of the afternoon passed in an ecstasy of physical love making. Eve was demanding but finally we dozed for a while.

Eve was up first again, dressed and making a cup of coffee.

'You know Eve" I called from the bed, "I did not think you cared much for me.'

'Did not care, are you for real? Patched your body up, took you in off the streets. Got you out of jail, brought you to the beach, for rest and recreation, let you have my body but I don't care. I think you need to rephrase that buddy boy. You're hardly a great romantic.'

'When you put it like that I think I'm a bit dim in the love stakes, always have been.'

We took dinner again that night at the Merryman Inn. It was as quiet as the previous evening.

'When I get back to Downderry I'm going to recce Gweebarra find a way in. If you would drop me in Liskeard tomorrow to check in with the cops, I'll get a taxi after to Kantara.'

'Not on your life buster' said Eve grinning. 'I'm responsible for you. If you're going to break the law we do it together, I'm in on the recce. What are we going to do?'

'OK then, if you're sure' I was glad she was so enthusiastic. Another pair of eyes would be welcome. 'We need a good map of the area around Gweebarra and the coast line, Ordnance Survey. Then we pick some high ground from which we can observe the house and grounds. And we watch them, see what the goons do. It still baffles me what they are doing there anyway. Perhaps they will have left. Important we reach the point unseen and cannot be seen going in and out as well. It will take several hours, best part of a day, could be quite boring for you Eve.'

'I don't think so, and if we do get bored we can always find something else to do.'

Her eyes danced with anticipation and joy, gone was the cold tint they sometimes appeared to have. There was something about this girl, Eve, which at times I found overwhelming.

'We need good visibility so we need to check the weather forecast. Do our homework.'

The next day, when we had returned from the north coast, she would drop me at the police station and then she had some duty to perform at Liskeard hospital, I would go onto Downderry. Eve had the evening surgery at Downderry after which she would spend the night with me at Kantara. Tuesday weather permitting we would set off for the recce.

That night our last on the north coast, the love making was not so frenzied, and afterwards we lay awake for some time just talking. Clasped together like two spoons in the narrow bed. I tried to find out more about Eve, her background in Canada, how she became a doctor. But she seemed unwilling to talk about it. She was more interested in the recce. What we needed to take, how long it might take. What we hoped to learn and how we might use it.

Finally her breathing became heavy and she was asleep. I lay awake wondering what our future might hold. But like Eve I kept coming back to the immediate task before us. The objective, lines of approach. It was good I was back beginning to think in military terms. It was skills forged in war never forgotten. Not when it really mattered.

But this weekend had been extraordinary with Eve, something else I would never forget.

Thirty-One

We were both up early. Within the hour had breakfasted and were on our way, heading back to the south east of the county. It was another glorious early summer's day with just the hint of a heat haze beginning high up toward the stratosphere.

In two hours we were back at Minions where Eve changed, refilled her weekend bag with clean underwear and jeans and shorts for the recce, and her stay at Kantara. It was just after eleven by the time she dropped me at Liskeard Police Station.

I checked in with the duty sergeant. 'Mr Nicolson, good' he said checking my name on a list.

'Yes Inspector Montague wants to see you. You're lucky he's here.'

Lucky, I did not think so. A WPC took me upstairs to Montague's office. It was more a den than an office. It reeked of stale tobacco smoke, and was as untidy as the Inspector was in his dress. On his desk was the picture of a pleasant looking woman, and two children.

'Nicolson, good of you to drop in, take a pew' he greeted me, taking the pipe from his mouth and resting it, still smouldering emitting thin whiffs of smoke, in a dirty glass ash tray. A stained cup sat on the desk. He closed the file he had been reading and placed it on a pile of several others.

I thought I had little choice but to '*drop in*' as he said, but said nothing.

'Good weekend with the doctor?'

'Great Inspector, but exhausting if you know what I mean.'

'I see Nicolson. I suppose you did not think of anything more about Bill Longman, being exhausted an all?'

135

'No sorry remains a mystery to me, but as I said before I hardly knew the man. Probably learnt more about him from my aunt's journals and that's not much even then.'

'Yes they were revealing. But I don't like MI5 down on my patch, don't trust the buggers they usually mean trouble.'

'And spending all this time looking after the Allan-Cleary's hardly seems right.'

'And for what reason Nicolson?'

'Surely the good major told you Inspector?'

'Said something vague about the IRA, but I don't think so. Got a pal in Special Branch and they have no inkling of anything going on down here in the South West, Nicolson. Do you think if Bill Longman thought the Allan-Cleary's killed your aunt, or were involved in her murder, he might have been willing to go after them? Have a go at them?'

'He was an old man Inspector, was he up to it?'

'Yes old, but still a crack shot. Served in the Auxiliary Units in the war. They were to act as guerrillas if the Germans had invaded in 1940, cutting lines, hindering supplies, picking off what targets they could. None of them had any illusions about their roll, or how long they would last. Theirs was a suicide mission. They did not stand them down until November 1944.'

Montague got up and walked over to his window which looked down onto the nearby fire station. With his back to me he carried on.

'A lot of those types of people are fanatics and I don't like fanatics, they're not normal.'

'OK Inspector he still had the skill and the field craft. So who killed him? Has to be the Allan-Cleary's in some way? And the way it was done I maintain had to be someone he knew or thought was not a threat.'

Montague came back to his desk. 'Which would seem to rule out the Allan-Cleary's. You see Nicolson you go around in circles like me. However forensics did come up with something. He was stabbed once in the back with a long thin bladed knife right up into the heart, died instantly. As if the murderer was trained to do it.'

'Do MI5 do that type of thing Inspector? Do they murder people with State approval, is there a licence to kill or is that just fiction?'

'I have asked myself that question Nicolson. And I have to admit to you now that perhaps your Aunt was murdered as well. As a copper I should dismiss it there is no evidence, other than the suspicions your aunt held, which is not evidence but?' He left the question hanging in the air.

He thought for a moment putting the stem of the unlit pipe in his mouth tapping his pockets for matches, and then removing it again to speak.

'You see I'm a government servant here to protect the public. I hate to think that another Government Department might conceivably murder, what amounts to their ex-employees just to keep them quiet and protect a stool pigeon. None of it makes sense after all these years.'

I felt sorry for the thoughtful Inspector. 'Could it be something else Inspector?'

'In what way?'

'Could it be they have got a whiff of something, that's how intelligence works sometimes? The 'something' might be a smoke screen.'

'What do you know about intelligence Nicolson?'

'Just from Northern Ireland, Inspector we used to get briefed by them there but half the time they were barking up the wrong tree and got things completely wrong.'

'No I think you are talking in riddles now. We must keep a clear head. The explanation when it turns up will be relatively simple, it usually is Mr Nicolson.'

'If that's all Inspector?'

'Yes, of course, good of you to share your views, don't let me hold you up. Much left to do with your aunt's estate?'

'No' I lied 'be out of your hair in a day or so.' I got to my feet.

'I suppose the good doctor is an incentive to hang about a bit longer' said Montague smiling 'lovely looking woman. Canadian isn't she?'

'That's right, good nature too.'

In Liskeard I got a reasonably powerful pair of binoculars at a camera shop. Two large green plastic ground sheets and a thermos flask at an ironmonger, an Aladdin's cave that seemed to have everything in it you might need, the building was dated 1858. There was little else we needed that I could not get in Downderry. I hoped Montague had not put a tail on me but saw no evidence of it.

By mid afternoon I was back at Kantara by taxi. Somehow I expected the bungalow to have changed, perhaps because I had, but it was just the same, almost accusing me saying 'what have you been doing, what about me?'

In the village I got a good map of the area and more groceries, an assortment of snacks for tomorrow, some steak for our meal that night, for I did not want to share Eve with anyone not on that night.

'Still with us?' said the woman behind the till in the Spar Shop.

'Yes, only a few more days now and all should be finished. The weather is glorious.'

'Yes and set to be for the next few days, that's what we want. It'll bring the visitors for certain this weekend.'

The weather part was what I wanted to hear.

Thirty-Two

At Kantara I opened up the ordnance survey explorer map for the Lower Tamar valley on the lounge floor. It gave me the wide expanse of Whitsand Bay, and to the east Plymouth Sound and the breakwater, and just what I wanted, Cawsand Bay I minutely studied the area around Gweebarra. The roads, the ground, cover we might use, high ground, routes of possible approach, and took notes on distances.

Then I went to the phone unscrewed the receiver and removed the bug carefully. Afterwards I dialled the number Kevin Harris had given me at Stonehouse Barracks knowing I would be lucky to find him on duty, but there was something I needed to check if possible.

A corporal answered, I told him who I wanted, he asked who I was, my luck was in, and he put me through.

'R N, how's it going?' said Kevin.

'Not bad boy'ho. Kevin I've got an odd question for you.'

'Alright' he said hesitatingly.

'Have you any idea of the Provo's operating in this area?'

'We are on Bikini Amber R N, but no buzz on any Provo cell.'

'Bikini Amber that's country wide?' Short of actual war it was the highest state of MOD alert.

'Yes all over. Have you got a sniff of something?'

'No not really, it's just something Inspector Montague said.' I decided not to tell him about Major Lanyon.

'So you are still down here?'

'Yes feet under the table with Eve.'

'Good on you. Anything on the Provo's for us R N?'

'No it's all rumours, nothing concrete Kevin.'

'We'll have to have a run-ashore soon R.N.'

'Look forward to it Kevin thanks oppo' and I rang off.

139

I replaced the bug in the phone, and in the kitchen switched on the radio to catch the early evening news while I peeled some potatoes.

'*A mass lobby by miners outside Parliament resulted in fighting and 120 arrests by the Metropolitan Police*' said the news announcer after a few minutes.

'*In Northern Ireland riots broke out in Belfast overnight. A military ambulance passing Kelly's Corner on the Springfield Road was petrol bombed. Two buses were hijacked in the Monagh Road and Crumlin Road and set on fire.*' Thus had passed a night I thought, of what went for normal in Belfast. I thought briefly of Eve's comparison to a civil war, perhaps she had a point with all that was going on.

At that moment Eve's head appeared around the back door.

'That's what I like to see a man at the kitchen sink.'

'Hello there' I said reaching over to the window sill and switching off the radio.

She kissed me on the cheek. 'Don't let me hold you up. I'll put my bag in the bedroom.'

'It's the one on the left I called after her. Water's hot if you want a bath or anything.'

Eve did not reply but I soon heard the water running into the bath. I thought about going into the bathroom, there was no lock on the door, to have a peek at that body. But it was funny, although we had been apart only a few hours I felt curiously shy again. After all we did not really know each other that well.

Eve soon returned in shorts and a T shirt. 'That's better' she said sitting at the kitchen table. 'I'm sure some of the patients never wash from one month to another. Did you get the gear Rob, the stuff you wanted?'

'Yes everything. Now do you want to eat sooner or later?'

'Perhaps we should look at the map before we settle down and get distracted.'

And so I went through it all again on the lounge floor for Eve. We formulated the plan which was to drive over to Mount Edgcumbe

Country Park, leave the car there. Take the coastal path back west to Fort Picklecombe, about a three mile walk, from where we would strike inland through wooded ground from the edge of which we would have a good uninterrupted view of Gweebarra, about four hundred metres away. Our approach using this route would be completely shielded from the house, mostly by trees and high stands of gorse. Tomorrow we would set off early and be in position before eight, and remain there most of the day. It all seemed over the top just to see a pensioner in a wheelchair.

We cooked the steaks, I found some garden furniture in the garage brushed and washed it off and we ate outside. It was a warm evening. Eve had brought a good bottle of Chianti with her which washed the steaks down well.

Afterwards we walked down to the beach and sat on the rocks, throwing stones at the sea saying little, and watched the sun sink in the west dipping into the sea, sending orange streaks racing across the surface.

Hand in hand we walked back to Kantara. Inside the front door Eve was in my arms quickly. My hands up inside the T shirt to her bare breasts, our love making was frenzied and then we slept, or I thought we did, for I woke and found Eve was not there.

I lay awake for a while listening for her return but finally fell asleep again. Presently she was waking me she was already dressed. Dawn had barely broken. We breakfasted on cereals.

'I missed you last night where did you get to?'

'Went for a walk, could not sleep, excitement I guess. This is all new for me.'

I had to admit the adrenalin was starting to flow in me it was something I had not done for a long while.

Thirty-Three

Before seven that morning we had parked the car at Cremyll and set off into Mount Edgcumbe Country Park for the coastal path, the park's sea of daffodils and blue bells were past their best now with spring gone. Plymouth's breakwater was so close it was as if you could reach out and touch it. Inside its protective arms two sleek grey Royal Navy frigates rode at anchor, we could see figures moving about the decks.

We walked on at a brisk pace, both carrying small rucksacks, largely in silence. I felt easy with Eve, there was nothing I needed to say. It was still cool and we made good time, the path was easy. After an hour we passed a shrine of the Virgin Mary with a small statue. Eve stopped crossed herself and bowed.

'I'm up for help from any quarter' she said.

I felt there was no real need for her to explain, obviously she did. I let it pass without comment.

Shortly we passed behind the grey granite of Fort Picklecombe, another of the Victorian forts that ringed Plymouth. Nearby we checked the map and soon struck inland on a steep path through high stands of gorse and rhododendrons. The gradient made us breath more heavily but it soon levelled out.

The path finally ran out and we moved on through stands of trees, finally reaching the end of the wooded area where open fields of grass lay before us. To the north was the spire of medieval Maker Church, away to the west we had a clear view of Gweebarra.

Keeping within the fringe of trees we laid out the ground sheets and unpacked our kit and had a cup of coffee from the flask and some biscuits.

To watch a position where nothing much happens can be boring, and you soon start to daydream. So you do it in small stretches of time. We decided to take it in turns in twenty minute periods, I took the first one.

Eve lay on her back quite close to me gazing at the sky chewing a piece of grass, but kept quiet.

Just before eight what I took to be the housekeeper or cook arrived on a moped. Obviously she did not live in. Gone were the days of the big staffs they had years ago in these houses, many of which in this area had been changed into country hotels or old people's homes.

Not long after that the brown Ford Cortina arrived and minutes later left again no doubt changing the guard. I still marvelled at the lengths they were going to, to protect the Allan-Cleary's, spending my hard earned taxes on such things.

Studying the house in some detail it did not take long to spot the CCTV camera's on four corners of the house positioned high up. Would they be infra-red, possibly, so at night we could be lit up like decorated Christmas trees.

The goons no doubt were in some control room where they could monitor the cameras. From there they had quickly spotted my direct approach along the main drive. There would be a camera covering that.

However using the binoculars to quarter the ground it did not take long to find a largely covered approach to the house. A hedgerow ran along one side of the length of the lawn which stretched almost to the sea four hundred metres away. I doubted the cameras had a range anything much over two hundred at best, and would be set looking down from their high positions covering a particular approach.

If we came in from the seaward side and moved toward the house keeping close to the hedgerow, keeping it between us and the house our movement would be completely shielded.

Until we needed to cross the hedgerow toward the house, which would mean barely a fifty metre dash, best done directly under the camera which in all probability would be too close to us, unable to depress any further they would be blind positioned too high, unable to see our approach or so my theory went. Probably like us only one of the goons would be watching, bored by the duty as well. I made some notes and then handed the binoculars to Eve. However the hedgerow was topped by nasty looking thorn, it would be like barbed wire, we would need long handled pruning shears or branch loppers to cut a way through, I wrote that down.

'Here you are your turn. Write down anything of interest as it strikes you' I said indicating the note book.

And that is largely how the day passed, with short stretches on the binoculars, we talked little.

About 2pm the brown Ford Cortina returned and quickly left again, the goons changing the guard. It still angered me the length MI5 was going to, to protect this old man.

It struck me then I knew little about the Allan-Cleary's background other than RP being a Nazi agent, what did I know? Martin was what, a hippy farmer and a bit of a local bully. And here was I about to enter the lion's den knowing virtually nothing about them. Or was I just getting cold feet? What did the target matter to a soldier, you just did your job.

'It may not be the time to bring it up but these Allan-Cleary's' I said lowering the binoculars, 'you know, I don't know much if anything about their background, they might shoot us on sight.'

'Well, I don't think I can help on that other than Gweebarra is a big bay in Ireland, so I should think they came from there. As to them shooting us I don't think so' said Eve, 'or I would not have volunteered. I'm not into putting my neck on the line.'

'Yep, I read that somewhere, I seem to remember they still have an estate over there. I suppose what I'm asking is how do they make their money, and own so much land. I think someone said, in the Inn-on-the-Shore, they own several farms in the area.'

Eve was right about them shooting us, RP was in a wheelchair, and Martin did not have the bottle. I took up the binoculars again.

'Does it really matter to us confronting them?' asked Eve.

'No I suppose not. What's this 'us' business Eve, you know more than likely this enterprise could turn out rough. I would rather do it on my own.'

'You don't think I'm letting you do this solo. I'm going to be right behind you buddy; after all I've signed for you.'

By the determined set of her chin I could tell this was not the time and place to argue.

144

The day dragged on. Overhead a buzzard hovered for some minutes looking out for some tasty prey below, and then floated away on the thermal layers. Later I saw him or another sitting on top of a telephone pole surveying his domain, with mechanical like turns of its head. The range of his eyes as good as my binoculars.

Late in the afternoon I broke the silence, Eve was watching the house, and we had already lunched.

'I think we need to come in by the seaward side. Then up by the hedgerow, over the hedge a short dash and we reach the house.'

'And how do we get in?' asked Eve.

'Probably through the French windows will be easiest' I recalled my aunt saying most of them had entered that way when they stormed the place in 1943.

'Will they be alarmed, the windows?'

'More than likely, but that might be enough to give old RP a heart attack anyway' which was not really what I wanted. We were merely there to make a demonstration 'The goons will probably be away from them in servants quarters, can't see they would have much in common or spending time together. It will give us a little time.'

I touched Eve's leg; she lowered the binoculars and turned toward me. 'You know we'll get caught, almost unavoidable, and arrested. You could get deported Eve and this is not your fight.'

Eve turned onto her back and gazed at me. For the first time I noticed one of her eyes was a darker blue-grey than the other, her left eye, I was drawn to it, into it. Her smile reassured me.

'Buster I am on the side of the small guy, the underdog, no matter what. I'm in this to the end. And it does not matter that much, I will be going home soon, my time's nearly up.'

'I will post the diaries off to Dad if the authorities get too bolshie we can always get the press on side, publish and be damned.' Although I had the idea I would try to publish them if I could anyway, that was what my Aunt had really wanted.

Eve turned back to watching the house, but continued talking. 'It's going to be a fair old hike to get in position by night, Rob. Why don't we get a boat and come into that little sandy cove?' She handed me the binoculars and pointed toward the sea.

It was easy to find what she meant. A tiny bay, a patch of sand between the brown grey rocks that looked like saw teeth stretching out razor sharp in places.

A small boat could reach it, and would be hidden from the house, once beached, by the height of the road between the house and beach that led on toward Fort Picklecombe and in the other direction toward the main road; hardly any traffic had used the road, just a post van that I could recall.

'What about a boat?'

"Think I know where I can lay my hands on one" said Eve.

We went over it again from every angle. So that became the plan.

We would come in at dusk, tides permitting; the sinking sun would be at our backs, we would be near invisible, low in the water. Ashore, movement to the house would be shielded by the hedgerow, once opposite the house we would cross over the hedgerow and into the house.

Even though the plan was settled we continued to watch Gweebarra. It was not long and the evening shadows were lengthening and we would soon pack up. It would be dark by the time we got back to the car over an hour's walk away.

I was about to stop watching when RP was wheeled out onto the wide veranda at the back of the house by Martin. I could not see his face, or Martin's, their backs were toward us.

I recognised Martin by his dirty knee length shorts which looked the same as the ones he had been wearing the last time I saw him. He left RP and went back into the house returning quickly with some drinks he placed on the garden table and sat on one of the chairs.

I guessed they were talking and handed the binoculars to Eve. 'Look at this.'

She studied them. 'So this is our quarry. Well let's hope they do this when we come it will make our task so much easier.'

After that we packed up and made our way back to the car.

Thirty-Four

It was late by the time we got back to Kantara. Eve pulled up outside but left the engine running. I reached toward the door handle but Eve did not move.

'Do you mind Rob; I'd like to go home tonight alone.'

'Of course not Eve', I lied 'It's been a long day and it will be another one when we move.'

'I need some sleep Rob that's all; I can't afford any mistakes in my job. I'll be around after morning surgery tomorrow and we'll sort out a boat.'

Eve kissed me passionately enough. I got out and she turned the car and drove away. She did not wave.

Of course, I told myself, as I watched her turn right at the end of the short street, it was hardly surprising. I was an insensitive dope. Kantara had witnessed two murders. Eve had to deal with dead bodies yes, but most had died from natural causes. Probably Kantara gave her the creeps. No wonder she had been unable to sleep. It tended not to bother me. After all, people killed people, not places. And I had known my aunt at Kantara when it had been a place of joy a good welcoming happy place.

Kantara merely yawned at me as I entered. I felt pretty wacked and went straight to bed. I did not even set any traps.

The next morning I woke refreshed, even managed some physical jerks out in the garden to loosen up a bit, followed by a good hearty breakfast. It was another warm summer's day with a high light heat haze. No doubt the tourists would be out in droves today, which would make the locals happy, listening to the ring of their tills, inflating their bank accounts.

In the village I got a tide guide; over the next few days the tides would suit us everything appeared ready to go. At the post office, I posted the diaries to my father. No doubt he would be unable to keep my mother and aunt from reading them, although I did mention the official secrets act in a letter I put in with them and only to reveal them to the press on my say-so, but by then everything would be settled, one way or the other.

Returning to Kantara my heart sank when I saw Inspector Montague's car parked outside, an old two tone Rover 100. What did he want now? There was no one in the car. I thought about retreating, waiting until he left. But he emerged silently behind me, it was only the smell of his pipe that alerted me, perhaps he had been speaking to the neighbours again.

'Ah Nicolson just the man, got a few minutes?'

'Anything for you Inspector, like a cup of coffee and I promise no condensed milk.'

'Thanks very much.'

We went in by the front door and I led him through into the kitchen and put on the kettle. He sat at the small table.

'So inspector, to what do I owe the pleasure? Can't imagine this is a social call?'

'Rich tea good-oh' he said indicating the packet of biscuits I had placed on the table with my other purchases that morning.

'Help yourself' I said handing the biscuits to him.

'Tide time table, thinking of fishing?'

'Might do Inspector or perhaps hire a boat.'

With his biscuits and coffee I felt Montague was here for some time. He was really the last person I wanted sniffing about this close to us moving on the Allan-Cleary's.

'I have done some checking on your theory that your aunt was murdered; always try to keep an open mind.' He then concentrated on soaking a rich tea in his coffee, then he withdrew it and held it in mid air while he talked again, I was sure it would break onto the table in a messy blob. I tried to listen to what he was saying.

'The Allan-Cleary's were not in Cornwall at the time your aunt died, they were at their estate in Ireland.'

Montague looked at the biscuit which he had held expertly intact, and then he consumed it in two quick rapid bites spilling not a piece and saying 'lovely.' Then licking his fingers. There was nothing much refined about him. But I had to admit a liking for the man. He then ferreted in his pockets finding at last a small note book which he opened.

'Yes they were at their estate in the Republic of Ireland, right up in the north about fifty miles from the border, called Halsgrove. Bigger than Gweebarra by all accounts, so they could not have murdered your aunt.'

'Surely it depends on their alibi Inspector, not that I'm trying to tell you your business.'

'Yes indeed, unfortunately for you it comes from the Garda, the local police. Martin Allan-Cleary was locked up at the time to cool his heels after some fracas in a pub over there I think. You see Nicolson they could not have done it.'

'Very convenient Inspector, they must have taken out a contract. Who was it said 'when you have eliminated the impossible, whatever remains, however improbable, must be the truth?'

'Arthur Conon Doyle, well his character Sherlock Holmes says it. It's possible but unlikely. They were in the grip of MI5, can't see it Nicolson.'

I had to admit myself I was beginning to have doubts.

'If it wasn't the Allan-Cleary's who was it? You see my problem Nicolson. Because then we have to find another motive. Which keeps me coming back to you and your aunt changing her will, good for you quite a bit of money involved.'

'No Inspector, the motive remains the same, my aunt's involvement with the Allan-Cleary's, somewhere in that lies the root of it, both murders. If you knew the rest of my family you would know I could never rob them through the will, that's a joke.'

'Perhaps' said Montague 'but rest assured Nicolson I'll find him, whoever he is.' With that he got to his feet, and I saw him out. At his battered Rover he stopped and lit his pipe.

'Keep in touch Nicolson' he said between puffs.

At that moment Eve drew up in the Triumph Spitfire with the hood down, she parked in front of the Rover and climbed out.

'I see the doctor's looking after you well' said Montague, drawing out the last word which sounded more like it meant *'interesting.'*

'Morning Doctor Reilly' he called. 'Glad to see you are still looking after him.'

'Surely, it's my civic duty Inspector' she answered Montague and then moved away.

Montague merely said 'Um' and started the Rover, turned in the drive, and acknowledged both of us with a wave of his smoking pipe and drove away.

Thirty-Five

'What did Montague want?' asked Eve.

I kissed her first. 'Oh the usual, barking up the wrong tree. I think he thinks I did in my Aunt and Bill for the contents of the will somehow, but he can't quite figure it out, somehow I got it changed, and he hopes I'm going to do a runner so he can pin it on me. He's got a shock coming to him.'

'Several people have a shock coming Rob that's true, and it sounds like Montague needs to go back to detective school.'

Eve looked bright and fresh even after a morning at the surgery.

'Let's go out for lunch Rob, I'll get the bill, and I think we'd better avoid the Inn-on–the-Shore for obvious reasons.'

'That's an offer I can't refuse, surprise me Eve' I said. With that I got my wallet and locked up Kantara, by which time Eve had turned the Triumph around and was waiting.

She set off through Seaton for Hessenford through the narrow tree lined Seaton Valley, and climbed the hill toward Looe, it was good with the hood down the fresh air all around us. Eve by-passed the fishing port of Looe, a favourite of tourists, and crowded by what we could see of it crossing the Looe River Bridge. At the village of Pelynt she pulled into the Jubilee Inn where we had a light lunch.

Having finished eating I asked. 'Where do you think we might find a boat Eve?'

She smiled at that. 'Got one lined up already a friend of mine in Seaton, I have borrowed it before. He will drop it down onto Downderry beach this afternoon. And then buster we are ready to go.'

I had to admire her resourcefulness, was there nothing beyond this woman? 'Well the tides are good over the next few days.'

'So when is D-day Rob, no point in hanging around?'

'D-day, or should we call it A.C-day. Just as well go tomorrow evening Eve, but I still worry about you being directly involved, I can do it alone you know.'

'No way buster I signed for you I'm doing my civic duty' said Eve. 'Tomorrow evening, that's good for me I need to go to the hospital in the morning then I'm all yours.'

The rest of lunch passed in a leisurely fashion, I probably drank too much. While Eve was on fruit juice.

Back at Downderry we found the boat already on the beach for us with a note attached just to give him a ring once we had finished.

'Does he realise the boat may be stuck over near Kingsand, Eve?'

'No worries I'll clear that with him, he's a real good friend.'

The boat was a twelve foot fibre glass job, light and strong, with an outboard motor and a couple of paddles, there were three life jackets. We unloaded most of the equipment into Eve's car.

I had to report to the police again although I had seen Montague that morning. Eve took me to Liskeard and afterwards we went onto Minions to spend the night together.

Eve cooked that night, a good light fish based pasta dish. Alcoholic drinks were kept down to just one glass of wine. 'We are in training' explained Eve. She had probably noticed how much I had drunk at lunch.

We watched the news on TV to catch the local weather forecast, the news was not good. A miner picketing a Yorkshire Power station had been run down by a truck and killed. Just another casualty of the Civil War.

Margaret Thatcher had hosted a meeting of seven major industrial nations for closer international cooperation against state-sponsored terrorism. She called for *"relentless action"* in the wake of the Libyan embassy siege in London followed by the killing of a police woman.

'A determined woman that one, quite ruthless' said Eve, I did not know if this was in admiration or loathing or was it both?

152

'About time too' I said 'give them a dose of their own medicine.'

'You have been doing that for years, you can't lock up a nation, or an ideal Rob.'

'The Nazi's would have shot them.'

'Which would make you no better than them.'

'You're a bit of a rebel I think Eve?'

'I suppose I am, but I told you that remember, and one man's terrorist is another man's freedom fighter. But don't take too much notice of me. Sit there and wait for the forecast.' She got up and took my plate with hers heading toward the kitchen, I soon heard the sound of dishes in the sink.

The weather forecast gave flat calm seas with light on shore breezes, ideal for our beach landing.

That evening we went for a walk out onto the moorland, amid rings of ancient standing stones we wondered;

'I bet these fellows could tell a tale or two' I said resting my hands on one of the granite uprights that must have weighed perhaps a ton or more. The surface was rough with smoother patches of moss and lichen. Funny the stones did not feel cold to the touch but warm. I put my ear to it and listened.

'Watch out Rob these are supposed to be female the most dangerous of the species, they were supposed to have been turned to stone for dancing on the Sabbath' she said, taking in the ring with a sweep of her hand. 'Mind you they date to the bronze age a long time before any Christian ever came here.'

'They don't have much to say' I said moving away from the stone. 'Do you think they will smile on our enterprise?'

'I doubt it Rob, what are man's petty concerns to them. Come on it's getting dark let's go back, and I need your body, some flesh and blood around me not long dead stones.'

So we returned to Minions and Eve's cottage.

Thirty-Six

The day, D-day, broke bright and sunny; below Minions mist curled and lingered in the valley bottoms. From here the land was laid out like a three dimensional map. The chimneys of the mine working engine houses stood starkly against the blue sky. Some five thousand people had once toiled here below and above ground, some in tented camps, a railway had wound its way up the mines, it hardly seemed possible. That was until it got too expensive to prize the tin and copper from the ground. Then the Cornish miners had gone to the four corners of the earth with their hard rock mining skills to wherever there was work. Many had also come to this place in the boom times, most from Ireland. I read about this in a booklet I found among Eve's magazines after she had gone to the hospital. Someone had underlined the part about Ireland and the Irish.

It was going to be a long day. A day spent waiting until evening. I thought about ringing my father to make sure he had received the diaries, but decided against it, it would raise too many questions that I did not want to answer at this time.

In the kitchen I listened to the radio, which told me Indian Troops had stormed the Sikh Golden Temple in Amritsar, after a four day siege. The temple, holiest of Sikh shrines, had been taken over by Sikh militants. There seemed to be fanatics everywhere. I tuned to a different station, and listened to some mindless pop music.

Eve returned mid-morning. We stayed at Minions until closer to lunch time. It would be of little use hanging around Downderry for too long. We were both largely silent alone with our own thoughts.

In Liskeard I got a good pair of long handled branch loppers in a garden centre while Eve sat in the car.

For lunch we stopped at the Copley Arms, Hessenford, where the Seaton River ran under a nearby small bridge, we took lunch without alcohol, lingering there until well past 2 p.m. and then finally drove on to Downderry.

Eve reversed the car down Beach Road close to the boat and we unloaded the gear into it. She parked the Triumph in Kantara's drive.

We had a cup of tea in the garden and we waited. Waited for 6 p.m. watched clocks and our watches, the estimate was it would take two hours to sail from Downderry east across to the small bay below Gweebarra. It was only a few minutes from there to the house where we should arrive about dusk. If we were early we could tread water out in Cawsand Bay. No one would take much notice of a boat there, just people out fishing.

My fingers began to tingle with anticipation and my stomach felt light. Adrenalin coursing around the body, it felt like it had when I had been waiting in the landing craft at San Carlos Water in the Falklands. It had been dark and cold, just the slap of water against the steel sides of the LCVP and the murmur of the diesel engines, waiting for the ramp to fall and to go into action. Then we were ashore on East Falkland. It was all before us those long exhausting yomps and the cold, always the wet cold. And night attacks filled with tracer crossing the sky, nights when men died, some in close fighting, and one particular Argie.

Eve was quiet, she lay on the grass her eyes closed but not asleep she answered questions briskly, in a clipped tone. No doubt she was feeling it too. Time passed slowly.

Finally, almost painfully 5.45 came. 'Time to go Eve' I said.

She looked over at me; we were still in the garden. 'At last I thought it would never come'said Eve.

We packed our gear, odds and ends, some hard rations, a flask of coffee, just in case. Binoculars, maps, a compass, the branch loppers, Eve had a small ruck sack.

We left Kantara by the front door; I was just closing the door with the key in the yale lock when the phone rang inside. *Blast* I thought *who was that?* I looked at Eve, her eyes were wide.

'Leave it Rob it can't be important.'

I nodded, she was right of course, I pulled the door closed and removed the key. Probably my parents I thought, mum more than likely, I could do without that now, of all times to ring. We had to remain focused on the task.

We walked away, for several steps I could still here the phone ringing insistently. Shortly we were at the beach having launched the boat into the flat calm blue green water.

Thirty-Seven

After attaching the outboard motor to the stern, I attacked the pull-start. One, twice, six times there was no sign of life from the engine. I checked the fuel supply was switched on and the tank was full.

'What's the matter?' asked Eve tersely. 'Do you want me to do it? Come on out of the way.' She was up rocking the boat, but I blocked her way. There was no way past.

I gave the motor another pull and it burst into life, settling, after I revved it on the twist throttle twice, into a steady tick-over. Eve returned to her seat in the bow.

'Steady now Eve, you can still...' I began.

'Look buster' she said turning toward me 'how many times do I have to tell you, I'm in this to the bloody end.' She turned away again. "Let's get going" a terse edge to her voice.

'OK all ashore that's going ashore' I said trying to lighten the atmosphere.

I lowered the propeller into the water and opened up the small engine on the throttle. There was soon a nice bow wave running and we headed out to the south east. About three hundred metres off the coast I turned more due east to follow the coast line to our objective, I checked my watch, and it was just after 6 p.m. We were bang on time. I throttled back the engine a little.

Out past Bass Rock, where you can see the coast road turn on a hair pin bend away from Downderry Village and inland. I tried to pick out Kantara but had left it too late. Behind us lay our white wake of disturbed water.

At Long Stone Rock, a great grey monolith, lying as if it had been thrown into the sea by a prehistoric giant, I turned the boat further out to sea. Away to the west was the hump of Looe Island.

To the west was Portwrinkle village with the granite gothic mass of Whitsand Bay Hotel at its heart.

'Where are you going Rob, France?'

'Firing ranges up ahead, give them a wide berth. Don't want to be shot by the good guys at Tregantle Fort.' I pointed out the fort above the sandy expanses of Whitsand Bay.

Eve nodded her approval.

I recalled so many range courses at Tregantle, on the SLR, Self Loading Rifle and GPMG, General Purpose Machine Gun, a windy spot, often having to allow for the wind deflection with your fall of shot.

After a few minutes I came back onto our easterly course. Well past Tregantle I closed the coast a little getting ready to round Rame Head, like the heel of a giant boot up ahead.

The sprawl of holiday chalets at Freathy Cliff, spreading east like a white and brown stain looked so out of place. What were the planners doing to allow that? Even the Battery at Whitsand Bay looked more in keeping. The only noise was the little engine and the slap of water against the hull.

We passed other boats but gave them a wide berth. Most were fishing, one or two diving on the wrecks that litter the bay's seabed.

Polhawn Fort another example of the Victorian military builders skill, now largely inhabited by rodents, came and soon fell astern. Then we rounded Rame Head with its coastguard station and tiny hermit's chapel. Our next outcrop was Penlee Point; I edged closer to the coast.

'Time check Eve' I said.

'Just after seven' she replied without turning.

I throttled back a little, we were well on course.

Another ten minutes and we passed close to the point with its fog station. Turning north into Plymouth Sound we could see our objective at last up ahead, and pick out the house of Gweebarra without binoculars.

'There it is Eve' I called. She merely nodded.

There was no doubt in my mind Eve had grown remote the closer we had got to this. She was not used to this stuff. I wished she had not come. She had already done so much to help and support me. Things might well turn out rough. This was perhaps too much for her. Maybe she would be better taking the boat back.

We had not discussed what might happen after the raid. No doubt the Allan-Cleary's would cry blue murder. Might even give the old man a heart attack. I fully expected to get into the house and could hardly wait to see the look on their faces, but equally did not expect to get out. Tonight more than likely would be spent in a police cell, perhaps Torpoint or Plymouth. Montague might turn up, waving his pipe stem at me 'thought you had more sense Nicolson, and now you have that lovely doctor involved,' I could hear him saying.

A vague plan had been discussed in case we did get out, taking the boat back to Cawsand, leaving it at the beach there overnight. Maybe staying the night in one of the pubs, in the twin villages of Kingsand and Cawsand, if not a taxi back to Kantara, and retrieve the boat the next day.

The low cliffs here were green with masses of ferns interspaced with stands of gorse, their flowers bright yellow. The rocks looked all brown and black and sharp. Away to the north-east was the great grey block of Plymouth Breakwater with its small fort. I concentrated on finding the tiny bay up ahead where we would land. Cutting the throttle back I picked up the binoculars, from that far out it took a little finding but at last I had it. The little bay was all clear, nobody sun bathing, fishing, or anything.

'Eve' I said getting up; she turned toward me 'take the binos and keep that bay in sight.'

She took them and adjusted the focus for her eyes. It took her a little while to find it.

'Got it' she said raising a hand pointing toward it.

Increasing the throttle I steered in toward the distant shore.

It was a tricky approach even on a dead calm sea with the fading light which we needed. Timing was crucial but we did not want to end up on those razor sharp rocks.

Away in the twin villages of Kingsand and Cawsand a few lights had already winked on, at Gweebarra no lights were visible.

Finally we came in between Sandway Point and Hooe Lake point marked on the map edging slowly in.

Eve gave directions, 'left a bit, right a bit' not all that nautical but effective all the same. I had to admit for the first time that day I was glad she was there.

At last the boat grounded on the sandy beach. I switched off the engine and raised the propeller. Eve was out on the beach already; having climbed out to join her we dragged the light boat well up the beach to keep it away from any tide in case we did not make it back.

'Well here we are all safe and sound' I said trying to lighten the atmosphere but Eve made no comment.

There was little we had to take with us, I took the binoculars and branch loppers Eve had her rucksack.

'Right let's go' I said, dusk was falling.

'Hang on Rob, sorry call of nature, I need a pee' Eve scurried away behind some rocks. She was back quickly.

'Ready now?' I asked putting as much concern into my voice as I could.

Eve nodded.

Thirty-Eight

I led the way across the beach to the road which ran from Maker Farm on toward Fort Picklecombe. It was the only exposed patch to the house we had to cover, that was if anybody happened to be looking, but it was only a matter of seconds we would be in the open. We ran across at a crouch. Strange how you always crouch in such circumstances covering ground like that. Often in news reels of troops advancing in war they are crouching, trying to make a smaller target keeping as low to the ground as possible, as if trying to weather a storm, as if they might get blown over rather than torn to pieces by shot and shell.

There was a light on now at Gweebarra I noticed; someone was there, a good sign. A gateway led onto the field, it was padlocked so we climbed over it. In the field we were beside the hedgerow well covered from view.

Walking upright beside the hedgerow we covered the ground quickly. In one or two places the ground was muddy where animals had been eating choice grass from the hedge or trying to shelter in shade from the biting horseflies. We soon covered the three hundred metres to the house.

Stopping, I clambered up into the hedge to get a better view through the thorn. The house was clearly in view. I could see people, two, out on the veranda, the Allan-Cleary's, my heart leapt. But we needed to go higher; I dropped back into the field.

'About another twenty yards higher, they are out on the veranda' I whispered close to Eve's ear. For we had no idea if they had sound on the cameras.

Eve smiled for the first time in hours, but her eyes were hard, cold grey blue pools, I had to look away.

Moving on Eve followed; stopping again here was an ideal spot, the thorn a bit thinner. We were covered from the veranda by the corner of the house and almost directly under the camera. In the blind spot it could not be depressed that far to see anything of us.

Climbing part way up into the thorn Eve handed me the loppers and I began work cutting a way through the hedge. It was like a barbed wire obstacle with its long spiky barbs longer than its metal equivalent.

Finally after some tugging and cutting my hands on the vicious barbs the way through was wide enough, handing the loppers back to Eve I wriggled my way forward. Suddenly I felt a sharp pain in my rump.

'Shit that hurt' I blurted out.

'Sorry Rob' said Eve, she sounded right behind me.

What did Eve have to be sorry about I thought but dismissed it?

'OK Rob move on it's out of the way now' said Eve.

Must have been a thorn spike I had impaled myself on. A little further and I was through and down the other side. Eve followed no longer carrying her rucksack.

Waiting at the bottom I helped Eve down then we ran over to the house flattening ourselves against it. My buttock still felt painful and I rubbed it.

'Ready?' I said.

Eve nodded.

Gingerly we made our way toward the end of the wall where the veranda started and ran the full length of the seaward side of the house, there our quarry was, suspecting nothing. Enjoying their drinks, but not for long I thought.

For some reason I could not comprehend I began to feel dizzy I shook my head and it cleared but in a few steps the dizziness came back.

Reaching the corner, I slumped down sitting, my back against the wall and I looked around it. There they were the Allan-Cleary's father and son, on the veranda drinking, watching the sunset.

At last I could tell them what I thought of the murdering bastards and soon the whole world would know the story. Their humiliation would be complete.

However for some reason I could not remember what I was going to say. Yet I had rehearsed it so many times. Trying to get to my feet my legs would not work, what was the matter with me?

Eve was standing before me. In her hand she held a pistol. It looked like a Walther but longer, with a silencer. She moved slowly past me, I tried to reach up to her but my arms would barely move. Briefly she bent down and lightly stroked my cheek but said nothing.

'Eve what are you doing?' I said or thought I did realising no sound came from me, my voice would not work. It was merely in my head.

With a huge effort of concentration I managed to twist my body from its sitting position, so that I was slumped lying on my chest in the open, but my head was turned and I could look along the veranda.

Eve was walking calmly toward the two figures who had not yet noticed her, the pistol held behind her back.

Waves of darkness threatened to engulf me. Shaking my head again my vision cleared but my attempt to raise my body was hopeless.

Martin had seen Eve; he was saying something his lips were moving he got to his feet.

Eve said something but I could not comprehend it, she brought the gun around I did not hear the thud of the silenced pistol but a hole appeared in Martin's head between his eyes. Blood trickled down his face and then his body folded and collapsed like a rag doll.

RP was desperately trying to turn the wheelchair. Eve moved around him to confront him, face to face.

'The Republican Brotherhood has condemned you to death. So die all traitors' she said loudly, no doubt so as he understood with his hearing aids what was happening and why.

Eve raised the gun close to his face; he brought up a thin shaking hand, was he pleading? The gun jerked in her hand and RP was pushed backward into his wheelchair his head flung back, his mouth open in some sort of soundless shriek but his eyes blank and dead.

Eve moved away I tried to follow her with my eyes to keep her in vision. But she soon disappeared, and I was falling, falling backward into darkness. I tried to hang on, to clutch at the stone work of the veranda. To hit it to use pain to keep me awake, but the darkness engulfed me in its embrace. Was this the sleep of death?

Part Two-Salisbury Plain.

Thirty-Nine

It was as if I was climbing a long ladder through a black tunnel upward. I guessed upward for I kept falling back, and then having to grope in the blackness for the ladder and starting all over again. Yet finally up ahead, as wearily I climbed one wrung at a time, there was a faint pin point of light I knew I must reach.

Eve did not kill me; maybe after all I had meant something to her. Something beyond her mission.

Twelve hours later swimming up through waves of darkness I emerged into the blinding light of a single bare 100 watt light bulb, in a police cell, my consciousness returned. In nauseus waves my head swam and ached as if someone from the inside was hitting it with lump hammers. So there I was once more at her majesty's pleasure.

A police sergeant I had not seen before told me I was in a Plymouth Station. A doctor had examined me, and I definitely was not allowed a telephone call. So much for individual liberty I thought.

'Bit of a stupid antic Nicolson' said Montague, arriving shortly after I had come to, 'thought you would have known better.' He filled the cell with his presence and pipe smoke.

'Don't blame yourself Inspector; you cannot be right all the time, not with people. Look at Eve; she took me in along with everyone else.'

'Not entirely Nicolson. Always do the paper work. When Eve Reilly, or whoever she really was, agreed to stand surety for you we checked on her, standard procedure. Unfortunately, we did it by post, can't blame anybody for that, we tend to believe what people tell us especially doctors and the like, and by the time Canada House replied, saying they had no record of a Doctor Eve Reilly from Toronto working here you had set off.'

'Funny I heard the telephone ringing as I closed the door at Kantara, thinking more than likely it would be mother.'

'No Nicolson that was me' said Montague.

'So Inspector, Eve killed Bill Longman and my Aunt, no doubt about that now?'

"Yes looks like it, Longman would have known her, trusted her like us all. She must have come to the door, wanted to find those diaries, I imagine she was trying to keep you out of her way at that stage. He led her into the house turned his back and she did not hesitate, he probably never knew what hit him. Long knife up under the ribs to the heart almost instant death, she knew what she was doing.'

'Maybe it was her brother Ian, Inspector.'

'Brother?' said Montague sitting beside me on the bed.

'Ian Reilly if that was his name supposed to be a newspaper man over here to cover the Miner's Strike or that's what he told me. Come to think of it they were both in the car that morning Bill got it.' And so I explained our meeting on Seaton Beach, Montague took notes not interrupting.

'And my Aunt?'

'Bit more difficult that one Nicolson. Your Aunt having been cremated, we will never know for certain. But with the security blanket on it they would never have allowed an autopsy even had she been buried, and would we have found anything? I doubt it. Probably she used some sort of injection, perhaps adrenalin even in a large dose would be hard to trace, would have finished your Aunt in minutes with the symptoms of a heart attack. Again your Aunt would have trusted Doctor Reilly.'

'You always think doctors are all about saving life.'

'Oh, I don't know. What about Crippen, or Josef Mengele, you get your murderers from all walks of life. And I've no doubt Eve Reilly thought herself as a soldier, a freedom fighter.'

'What now Inspector?'

'It's all been hushed up, never happened, official secrets, MI5 on the job, out of our hands. I'll try and find out what they have in store for you.'

Montague left the cell. The Sergeant returned with some aspirin for my head, and lunch, same basic fare as the Liskeard Police Station, the cook here must have attended the same culinary school. Down to getting whatever it was into the same congealed mess.

'Looks like you're going to an ex-army camp up country closer to London' said Montague on his return; he sat beside me on the bed. 'You will be de-briefed there as they put it.'

'Do you know what she gave me?'

'Some sort of powerful sedative in the rear.'

'Oh, I know where it went in alright, it's still sore' I said nodding. So that had been the thorn on the hedgerow or what I took to be the thorn. A hypodermic needle instead, probably had it in the rucksack along with the pistol. And that explained her 'sorry Rob' when she did it, her bedside manner. I laughed at that, shaking my head which I quickly stopped as it started the hammers off. What a fool, it was me who had got her into Gweebarra. Montague must have read my mind.

'Don't be too hard on yourself Nicolson, she took a lot of us in, clever people, and these groups, whichever one she came from are so patient time means nothing to them. And she took a big risk she must have known we would check her background, gambled we would be slow. By the sound of it, through health services checks, she must have been a doctor, she knew her onions.'

'Or bodies' I said.

'Or bodies as you say Nicolson. I don't expect we'll meet again' said Montague, standing and extending a hand.

I stood and took his hand. 'So Inspector, happy I guess; now you have solved the case.'

'That's right Nicolson but then I usually do.'

Forty

Early the next morning, before light, two goons took me in a Ford Granada to a camp on Salisbury Plain, somewhere east of Stone Henge which we passed not long after dawn. Mist curling around its ancient stones.

Home became a featureless camp, a group of nissen huts of World War Two vintage, surrounded by high link wire mesh fences topped by rolls of barbed wire. Some had been used for prisoners of war. I had stayed in similar places during my time in the corps when on exercise on the plain.

They put me in a secure room there which was marginally better accommodation than the police stations I had recently had the pleasure to stay in. There were windows and something to look at, other huts. The food was marginally better, or was it that I was getting hungry. It took two days for my head to completely clear.

The goons told me nothing other than the same line, waiting for debriefing by a senior officer. In other words they did not know what to do with me, or even if I had been in on it all along. I was allowed to exercise walking around the camp with a couple of minders, for an hour a day. The plain here was largely featureless only the odd stand of trees away in the distance. No other buildings were in sight. No squaddies out there playing soldiers as far as I could tell.

It was no real surprise to see Major Lanyon again at my debriefing. He was there with two other officers who were not introduced to me.

One about the same age as Lanyon with long greasy hair, the other older, did age mean rank? One thing about him perhaps in my favour, he wore a Royal Navy tie.

In the interview room we sat at a round table. So the 'them and me' element was reduced or were they really that sophisticated, or maybe that was the only table they had. A more likely explanation.

When I arrived Lanyon greeted me like some long lost friend. 'Ah Nicolson, good to see you again.'

Somehow I doubted that but nodded toward him merely saying 'Major', and sat down without being invited to do so.

'I'm in the chair knowing the case, Nicolson, all informal. These gentlemen are merely observing. So what happened down in Cornwall Rob, start from the beginning?'

That was the first time Lanyon had used my Christian name, it put me on guard. But I told the whole story again leaving nothing out, I wanted to get back to normal away from these people if I was to be allowed to.

'You have no idea who Doctor Eve Reilly, or her so-called brother Ian Reilly, said Lanyon, really were?'

'None Major, I took her for what she appeared to be, a Canadian Doctor, on loan, to the NHS, or whatever they call it. Inspector Montague did some checking he was pretty sure she was a real doctor, but checked anyway as you know. So she took him in too, to start with. Her brother I only met twice. But as I think about it now it is obvious he came to find me the second time at the Inn-on-the-Shore'

Lanyon merely nodded and glanced at Long Hair.

'The Republican Brotherhood has condemned you to death. So die all traitors to the cause. You're sure that's what she said when she shot the Allan-Cleary's?' said Long Hair.

Was there a slight tinge of an Irish accent about him? I thought so. I did not like the look of him he looked mean and slightly bored by the whole proceedings.

'Yes I am, the sedative was working but I put a final effort in before I passed out. And it stuck in my mind, yes she said it alright. I did not dream it. Who are the Republican Brotherhood anyway, never heard of them before?'

'The Irish Republican Brotherhood, forerunner of the IRA, highly secretive, Michael Collins led it during the Anglo-Irish war at the end of the First World War. The name is hardly used these days, or we did not think so' said Navy tie.

Long Hair got up and lit a cigarette, walked over to a window and opened it but remained there looking out the window smoking.

'We have a whisper' said Lanyon 'it might be used by a US branch now. A lot of Republicans over the years have gone there, told to leave Ireland, deported you might say. Do you think Eve Reilly might have been a yank?'

'Could be, hard to tell the difference' I said.

'Yes of course' said Lanyon.

'Bit stupid on your part Nicolson' said Navy Tie ' telling your parents to go to the press with those diaries. The editor of the paper, any paper come to that in this country, had no choice but to call us in, when he read all that about naval intelligence.'

'It might have been better if you lot had taken me into your confidence instead of acting like bully boys. If you had told me RP had not only spilt the beans on the Nazi's, but the IRA as well I might have understood.

I was only trying to fulfil my Aunt's wishes, exposing RP as a traitor. Don't you people trust anyone? If you had told my Aunt she might have acted differently as well. And what were you doing down there with the Allan-Cleary's anyway?' They were beginning to annoy me with their secrets.

Navy Tie raised his eyes to Lanyon across the table as if saying 'your question Major.'

'You have a point Nicolson, but our operating procedures are on a need to know basis. Tried and tested over the years.'

'Oh come Major, I think Nicolson can be told as the bird has flown' said Navy Tie. 'We were using Allan-Cleary as bait, there are several IRA groups operating in this country we put it about he was a double agent trying to bring them out. Worked in a way but turned out a complete balls up. Months of work down the drain. Have you any idea where this person the doctor' he glanced down at the file in front of him 'this Eve Reilly might have gone?'

'None at all, she told me little if anything of her background, I know why now. And you are telling me you were using Allan-Cleary as bait for the IRA after forty years. I didn't think they had much to do with the War?'

"What do you think they re-emerged out of the Irish bogs with the troubles in the sixties Nicolson?' Long Hair said, irritation in his voice, he returned to his seat.

He continued, 'Five days before the invasion of Poland the IRA bombed Broadgate in Coventry killed five people and injured fifty. The IRA was already on a war-footing.

The Abwehr and the IRA tried to get together in the War a few times usually with no success. They never quite trusted each other. And the IRA was generally squabbling among themselves. Allan-Cleary was recruited in 1935 by the Abwehr as a fringe member of the IRA. He joined the RNVR as a sleeper. Later he learned from the Abwehr about the IRA cells in the UK, as contacts, it was them he betrayed, and kept betraying until they found out.'

Navy Tie nodded and closed the file on the table and that was basically the end of the de-briefing. I went back to my room accompanied by my minders.

For two more days I stayed there. Three meals a day, exercise with my minders around the camp. Locked up at night. No news from the outside world.

Then Lanyon and Long Hair came to see me again, we sat at the same table. This time I went through books of mug shots, looking for Ian Reilly. I never expected this to work. People did not have that good a memory. But after about an hour and mid way through the third book there was who I knew as Ian Reilly staring back at me.

'That's him' I said 'no doubt in my mind.'

'Let's see' said Long Hair. I passed the book to him and he went through some index in the back.

'He is an Ian, Ian Kagan, born Southern Ireland Tralee on the west coast 1951. Arrested 1977 by the Garda, on Terrorist activities shooting at British troops across the border. Clever lawyer got him out. However compromised then disappeared likely to North America. To set up a cell there, an operational commander.'

Lanyon nodded. 'Probably supplied the gun for the doctor.'

'You say he told you he was over here to cover the Miner's Strike as a reporter? said Long Hair.

'That's right.'

'Hmm' said Long Hair 'some of these types canny keep quiet. There was talk about the Provo's trying to stir trouble in the strike, worth checking out Major.'

'Could be' said Lanyon.

Long Hair picked up the photo books and left the room without a word.

'Thanks for your help; you're free to go Nicolson, a lucky man. We will be keeping your Aunt's diaries for the time being. Here you are' he handed me a rail warrant. 'I'll get one of the men to drop you into Salisbury Station. Remember you have signed the official secrets act, all this never happened.'

'Major I want to forget all about it too. And as to being lucky, yes I was how close to death do you think I was?'

'With Eve Reilly you mean? Pretty damned close I should say Nicolson.'

I did not need the Major to tell me. When I had realised that it made me physically sick, I felt I had been in the clutches of a black widow about to be consumed. It gave me nightmares for a while. Yet at the back of my mind I found it hard to believe, after the weekend in the caravan, that she ever meant to kill me.

'Good Nicolson, well I think you have everything. Have you ever thought about a career in intelligence? We can do with people like you. Resourceful, bit of a maverick.'

'No I don't think so Major; I like to know what I'm doing.'

'Even if it's counting bin-bags or whatever you do at that council Nicolson?'

So we were back to surnames I noted, not that it mattered. 'Yes, even that Major, it seems positively attractive from where I'm standing now.'

Forty-One

The first few days back at home were difficult. Hard to explain what had happened without going into too much detail. As much was still covered by the 'Official Secrets' and some in the family were not capable of keeping any secrets official or otherwise.

Mother, as I knew, was the most persistent. But even she, after time, gave up against my stonewalling. And my Mother and Father had been visited by an intelligence officer, not Lanyon, but a Captain Hancock, about the diaries which had been handed over to MI5 by the Newspaper Dad had given them to. They had been told that I was 'helping them with their investigations', which to a degree helped pacify my Mother.

My Aunt's estate was sorted, after a few months, and I duly signed over Kantara with all its contents to my parents which helped settle things down. They duly, after some thought with Aunt Karen and family conferences, which I avoided, put Kantara up for sale. I kept the contents of my Aunt's bank accounts about two thousand pounds. After what had happened and my loss of pay from the council for taking several days of unpaid leave it did not seem unreasonable. With that chunk of money I bought an MG Midget in British-racing-green and paid a good bit off the mortgage on my flat. As no one seemed interested in the bungalow at Kantara on Cyprus I ended up with that too. Like some sort of booby prize.

Life back at Merton Borough Council soon returned to what was normal. My immediate boss was as obnoxious as usual. And the fact MI5 had cleared my absences at the highest levels of the council did not help either. He would have liked to sack me.

With a car now, it was easier to pick up women, who out-numbered men at Merton Borough Council offices by four-to-one.

Soon I was tied up with Dawn, young even for me, not yet twenty, but demanding which was perhaps what I needed after Eve. It was not so easy to forget Eve. She had got under my skin, I dreamt about her sometimes. Not in any horrific way either. Just normal everyday things.

The country simmered on through the summer. A bolt of lightning set fire to York Minister, which the Church of England claimed not to have been an act of God. The Los Angeles Olympics, which the Eastern Block did not attend, came and went.

The whole country was staggered by the IRA bomb attack against the Tory Conference HQ, at the Grand Hotel Brighton. They had tried to blow up the Government. Four were killed in the rubble but they just missed the Prime Minister. The IRA gloated. Releasing a statement; *'Today we were unlucky, but remember we have only to be lucky once.'* Dazed cabinet members and MP's wandered aimlessly around Brighton front in their smouldering dusty pyjamas as firemen searched the wrecked hotel for bodies while fearing more bombs. That was on a Friday in October, I wondered had the caper in Cornwall been part of a distraction plan is some way. The IRA was quite capable of sophisticated operations and thought years ahead sometimes.

And the Miners Strike ground on, with more violent clashes this time at Maltby Colliery.

Part Three-San Francisco, California.

Forty-Two

The IRA blew up the Tory Conference on Friday 12 October, on the following Tuesday Major Lanyon phoned me at work.

'Nicolson, Lanyon here.'

I knew his voice instantly. 'Yes' I said hesitatingly.

'Need to see you old man, just a follow up interview, come around tomorrow.'

'I'll have to see, Major, if I can get the time off, where are you?'

'Already arranged with your people at the Council', he chuckled 'come around to the main offices on Gower Street. Bring some I.D., driving licence, and passport, something like that you know the score. Ask for me at the main desk. Ten sharp tomorrow, goodbye.' With that the dialling tone was droning in my ear.

My boss at the Council was bordering on the furious, but could do nothing everything went on way above him.

'What are you up to Nicolson?' he said trying to pump me. He was itching to know.

'Sorry, not cleared and need to know, old man' I replied, and realised I was beginning to sound more like Lanyon myself.

Dawn was a bit more difficult when she found out I would not be at work tomorrow. She did not stay with me all the time, usually only weekends. No doubt she suspected another woman. She had asked me once who Eve was, as I had called out her name in my sleep. I denied I knew an Eve, saying she must be just a dream character. Perhaps the original Eve in the Garden of Eden, original sin and all that I joked hiding my real Eve, locking her away.

Eve still haunted me. She was like a dark night of the soul; enveloped in a fog of betrayal and death. Perhaps it was that she had been emotionally, if not sexually, uninvolved with me. Perhaps it was an ego thing, what had I really meant to her? Was I just a tool? A question now that would never be answered.

Surprisingly Mother liked Dawn even though she was so young. She saw in her a kindred spirit who would tie me down. I would get married and have children with Dawn everything would be normal. Who knows that might have happened had it not been for Major Lanyon's call.

I lied to Dawn, saying I was attending an old Commando Unit reunion, I suppose it was not so bad, for in a way I was.

The building on Gower Street, HQ of MI5, not far from Euston Road underground station and in the direction of Trafalgar Square, was hardly imposing standing between a Further Education College and a hospital. A policeman in the reception area, with a row of medal ribbons on his chest, took my name and scrutinized my driving licence. Then consulted a list, finding my name he pinned a plastic tag on me and I signed a register. A reception flunky in a blue uniform also with medal ribbons led me to the lifts in which we went up to the third floor and then through a labyrinth of corridors. He passed the time of day with me, about the weather, and his views on Tottenham Hotspur's next home game. Finally he opened a door with a, 'here we are sir;' it led into an office containing a secretary who looked up.

'Hello Reg' she said.

'Mr Nicolson for the Major, Julie' he said and left.

Julie was a rather portly, pretty middle aged woman.

'Please take a seat Mr Nicolson' she indicated several arm chairs 'you are good for time, the Major likes that' she spoke softly into an intercom.

From this office a door led off on both sides, to other offices. I wondered which one was Lanyon's. Obviously he shared the plump Julie so he was not that high up the tree, not having to share a secretary. He did not keep me waiting long, emerging from the door on the left.

'Hello Rob' he greeted me, 'good of you to come over' his dark eyes beamed.

That put me on the alert, back to Christian names, that meant he wanted something only I could supply but what? This was more than a mere follow up interview.

'Come into the Den' he said stepping aside to let me enter first. 'Julie can we have some tea in about ten minutes please?' then he followed me.

Lanyon's room was big with a large well polished desk in mahogany, on which sat two telephones one red one green, the latter looked like a scrambler, I wondered if he had phoned me on that one. There was a safe, some filing cabinets and one wall was floor to ceiling book shelves, holding leather bound books. The big window looked out onto the back of the building. The desk was bare except for a single unopened file. I could not read the cover, it was too far away, but assumed it was mine.

'So how has it been, completely recovered?' he asked the black eyes studying mine intently, his thin blond moustache twitching slightly.

'Fine Major.'

'Any repercussions from the Cornish business?'

'None really, bit of flack at work wanting to know about my powerful friends. But easy enough to deflect, smoothed things over with the family, my late Aunt's estate broadly sorted out now. Thought you fellows would be busy with the Brighton Bombing now, not wanting to see me?'

Lanyon smiled thinly. 'Yes we are, but the local police were responsible for security. We have just got to try and catch them now. Mind you there could well be changes after this, changes to the remit; people might start listening to us.'

'You don't think that business down in Cornwall was just a smoke screen, cover in some way?' I said.

'Disruption you mean Nicolson, may have been. The IRA is always trying to stretch us all the time, leave us thin on the ground. It is a constant battle which is why intelligence on them is vital.'

With that Lanyon opened the file; he slipped a post card from it across the table. 'What do you make of that Nicolson?'

The card was one of those that are split into four pictures in the centre was a ships rescue ring with *'Fisherman's Wharf San Francisco'* emblazoned on it, one of the pictures was Pier 39 a seagull stood on a wooden pylon of the pier. I don't know if Lanyon noticed my intake of breath. Turning it over all it said printed in capitals was *'SORRY ROB'*. It was addressed to me at my flat in the same printed hand.

'So you have had my mail intercepted Major?'

'Yes standard procedure in this sort of thing, do it for twelve months or so, for your protection. Just following up.'

I raised an eyebrow at that one. 'Pity you don't pay my bills while you're about it.'

Lanyon ignored that comment. 'You're thoughts on the card Nicolson.'

'The postmark is Austin Texas, posted over a month ago' I said.

'I know that' said Lanyon irritation creeping into his voice, 'do you think it's her?'

'Could be Major, now I think about it Pier 39 did come up once. We were talking about favourite restaurants; hers had once been on or near Pier 39, coincidence?'

'In my business we don't believe in coincidence Nicolson. And you omitted to tell us about this conversation, about the restaurants?'

'Completely slipped my mind, the card has just brought it back.'

'Do you know anybody else out there, or in the USA as a whole?'

'No Major, I suppose given the circumstances it has to be her.'

'That's what we thought and then this came in.'

The Major slid an eight by ten black and white photograph across the table. I picked it up; it was grainy, taken in what looked like a hospital corridor. A woman dressed in white doctor's two piece overalls, a stethoscope around her neck was moving toward the photographer, she was off centre in the frame. Obviously a hidden camera, the subject had no idea what was happening. The face looked similar, a bit fuller perhaps; her hair was different, longer, almost to her shoulders and dark brown or black. The overalls hid too much of her body for any clues there, I could not tell who it was. It could be any woman.

'You think this could be Eve Reilly, Major?'

'We don't know but the FBI watches the IRA, they don't like terrorists operating from the good old USA, going abroad to spread death and mayhem. This person they believe is involved with the IRA operationally.' He glanced down at the open file. 'Calling herself Scarlett Maloney. We believe we hung her grandfather in Belfast in 1943 on information gained from RP Allan-Cleary. There are just too many coincidences stacking up, makes me uneasy.'

'Yes I see but I'm sorry Major I cannot tell from the picture.'

'No didn't think you would be able to. So we want you to go over there, take a closer look. If it's her we can extradite her, might learn a lot about their operation over there and here.'

'And then lock her up for life Major? Or will it be another deal?' Yet, here might be an opportunity I thought, I might be able to put my ghosts to rest at last.

I studied the photograph again looking for some clue. The Major handed me a magnifying glass, it made little difference.

'No good Major it's not close enough.'

'Will you do it Nicolson, go over there?'

'Why not, I've never been to San Francisco.'

'Good man, you're booked on the morning flight from Heathrow, all cleared with your people, and should only take four or five days.'

With that Julie entered with a tray of tea things.

'Ah! Tea' exclaimed Lanyon. 'Well done Julie, rock cakes as well' he rubbed his hands with glee.

Julie poured the tea for us then left. I noted it was not condensed milk here.

'Help yourself to cakes Nicolson' said Lanyon tucking in and scattering crumbs on the floor.

It was me this time, brought us back to the subject of Eve. 'Am I right in thinking Eve, or Scarlett, works in the hospital pictured?'

'Yes indeed, St.Mary's it's called. The oldest working hospital in the city, the Sisters of Mercy, from the Convent of Mercy in Dublin, started it. Eight nuns went over in 1854, went with the gold prospectors, pretty rough place San Francisco then. The building used now is on Stockton Street. So you see it has a long Irish Catholic connection.'

'You're not suggesting the hospital recruits for the IRA?'

'No, of course not, just that it has that Irish background. A firm connection old man.'

'Do we know where Scarlett Maloney lives Major?'

'Yes on Clement Street' he said glancing at the file 'in the Richmond district. Her flat or apartment as they call it was held by her while she was over here. Rent, bills paid everything, according to the FBI.'

'Do we know she was over here.'

'No that's a guess, her mail was redirected to Canada, and so her coming from Canada was a good cover story.'

"Anything else on her Major, what about her so called brother Ian, what was his real name again?'

'Ian Kagan, as far as we know he did go back to Canada. Have no leads on him in San Françisco or the USA as a whole.' He brushed crumbs off his suit.

'No news on either one but the FBI, and our man over there, Andy Peters will take care of you.'

'Andy Peters, our man in San Francisco' I said trying to inject some humour into the conversation.

'Yes I see' said Lanyon.

But I do not think he did.

'Julie will look after you now Nicolson. Tickets, money and things all her pigeon, you're passports up to date we checked' he said, while guiding me toward the door. 'I'll see you when you get back old man.'

And then I was outside in the capable hands of Julie.

Forty-Three

The next morning I left a grey overcast London on the BA scheduled flight to San Francisco International Airport. It had not taken me long to decide against telling the family where I was going and maybe, as it was only four or five days they might not even miss me. Looking at my watch it was nine fifteen, we were still gaining height flying over Ireland. By now Dawn would be at her desk in the housing department and would know soon that I was not at work; that would take some smoothing over with her. However, I soon dismissed those matters from my mind, what counted now was Eve Reilly, or Scarlett Maloney, or whoever she was. And more important how to handle it, if I got my chance to see her alone.

Ten hours later I arrived for the second time in the United States, the first time had been on a RN aircraft carrier arriving in Florida for joint exercises with the US Marines in South Carolina. But this was my first time to the west coast, to the Golden State.

Passing through US Immigration was fairly straight forward. Apart from some confusion over my occupation, the officer thinking working for a local council meant I was some sort of lawyer. In the end I gave up trying to explain and agreed I was a lawyer. He stamped my passport with a jovial: 'Have a good stay councillor.'

In the concourse, I held a rolled up copy of the London Times in my hand as a recognition signal. Julie had told me to carry the newspaper; I could hardly believe it, thinking it only happened in books or films. I need not have bothered for I soon found Andy Peters holding up a card with my name on for everybody to see. Well that was good security I thought.

We shook hands. 'They told me to carry this' I indicated the Times.

'Oh that old one what a lark', he grinned. 'Come on Nicolson let's get out of this scrum. I have a cab waiting outside for us; we'll soon have you at your hotel in The City.'

Andy Peters was a man of about forty, his sandy hair beginning to thin, and a bit overweight. He wore glasses, behind which friendly intelligent brown eyes examined me. Wearing a tweed jacket with elbow patches he looked more like a school teacher rather than, what, a spy? Did they call them spies? I wondered what they put down as an occupation, probably civil servant.

In the yellow cab, Peters filled me in on some details. He lived at Berkeley, and to my surprise did teach English Literature at the university and was a part time spy. That told me something about the priority London had given to Eve.

'So the target' I said, trying to sound professional 'lives on Clement Street out toward the hospital where she works as a doctor.'

'That's right but we have to wait for the FBI on this one, I don't think they have given this a high priority. Don't worry it's all on expenses, do a bit of sightseeing. It's a wonderful city lots to do.'

Peters sounded more like a tour guide now. I had hoped he might have given me Eve's full address. Looking at Clement Street on a street map of the city it was a long one. For it was in my mind now I wanted to see Eve alone. Not to go spying on her, or go bursting in with all guns blazing. Strangely I wanted to know her again, to get her out of my system. It was the only way.

Peters dropped me at the Cathedral Hill Hotel on Van Ness Avenue, with a cheery: 'Great Hotel this Rob, I'll be in touch, check with the hotel desk before you go out and come back for messages. You know the routine. Otherwise, as our colonial friends say, have a nice day.'

Climbing the steps of the grand entrance of the Cathedral Hill Hotel, it took me a little while to work out who Andy Peter's 'colonials' were. It must have been the jet lag.

My room was on the 8th floor. I unpacked and had a long warm shower, which helped refresh me from the flight.

Standing with a towel around me in the bedroom I had a good view over the city and bay. Tiers of white houses marched before me in neat rows to the waterfront; Pier 39 was somewhere down there. Alcatraz, the high security prison on its island, now abandoned and drab looking, was a favourite with tourists. I read in *A Guide to San Francisco* supplied by the hotel that in its heyday it had held Al Capone and Machine Gun Kelly. I yawned at that tossing the guide away onto the bed. So what that was not why I was there. Away to the west at the entrance of the bay was the Golden Gate Bridge, all red and bright in the sun. Should it not be shrouded in fog? That's how it was often portrayed. However, all this failed to absorb me; all I could think of was Eve.

First, after dressing, I went in search of food. I had a steak sandwich and a beer in the hotel bar.

'I have a friend over on Clement Street' I asked the bar tender, a young man with a friendly face of Mexican descent, 'but stupidly I have come away without her number, any way I can find out?'

'Surely sir, if I were you I might check out the phone book, plenty in the phone booths in reception.' It was so obvious. I thanked him with a good tip. Perhaps it was jet lag slowing down the brain cells again.

There were a lot of Maloney's in the book, over a page of them. But only three on Clement Street and only one S.Maloney at 482, it had to be Eve, for some reason I could not call her Scarlett. She was Eve to me. I wrote down the house number and phone number, and the number of St.Mary's hospital as well. But even then I doubted an IRA assassin would be in the phone book. Yet she was a doctor first and foremost.

Taking a newspaper from the lobby I returned to my room. Sitting on the bed I looked at the phone and explored my options. Should I ring her? No I decided, I had to see her face to face, and maybe the FBI would have bugged her phone. Surely they must have. But I could not merely go there and sit on her doorstep.

So instead I tried the hospital, I rang and asked if Doctor Scarlett Maloney was on duty, I gave my name as Matt Sebastian, the name of an article writer in the paper. I expected the standard; *'we cannot give out that information'* but instead I got 'she was not on duty today, perhaps I might ring back or could another doctor help me' I put the phone down. The chances were she had to be at home. I could not wait, to be certain. Sooner or later Andy Peters and the FBI would turn up. I had to see her alone. Time was not on my side.

There was a cab outside the hotel; I took it to 482 Clement Street. I did not check reception for any word from Andy Peters before I left.

The trip took ten minutes. The streets were arrow straight, and after the steep climb from Cathedral Hill flat.

The house where I was dropped was a white block of four apartments. Her name S.Maloney was behind a plastic strip beside one of the four bells inside a small lobby, it looked like it was an upper floor apartment. I rang the bell, there was no reply. I waited ten minutes and tried again, no reply. Across the street were some shops, I walked over to them. There was a cafe from where I could watch the house. I went in.

I made the coffee last an hour, but nobody entered 482 Clement Street. It was past four pm. I thought about returning to the hotel, getting some sleep, which I needed, and trying tomorrow but she might be on duty at the hospital then. And the FBI might put in an appearance any time. Having noticed a large second hand bookstore on the street, I moved on there to pass more time, in the hope Eve would turn up.

Another hour went past. The staff took little notice of me; it was harder to keep an eye on the house from this shop, and to apparently take some interest in the books. Finally I picked up a facsimile edition of *'The Great Gatsby'* I felt I should buy something. Making my way around a tier of book shelves toward the till I saw her. She was in the book shop. She did not see me; I ducked back behind the shelves, and took another discreet look through a gap in the shelves.

There was no doubt in my mind, she might have longer black hair instead of blonde but it was her. Perhaps it was the tilt of her head or

186

the way she stood, it had to be her, and it was her voice. I felt strangely lightheaded. Not apprehensive as perhaps I should.

Eve was chatting with the shopkeeper, a young man in sandals, shorts and a T shirt, looked more like a hippie than a book shop owner. They were talking about the weather, not looking forward to the cold damp winter. Perhaps they might manage a few days in Hawaii. He gave her some change and the book she had bought wrapped in a paper bag, and; 'Thanks Doctor Maloney, you have a good evening now you hear' he said in a southern drawl.

Forty-Four

'That's a good edition' said the hippie southerner 'facsimile of the original jacket and all.'

'Was that Doctor Maloney I saw just now?' I asked, getting my wallet out to pay for the book. Having watched Eve leave the book shop and turn in the direction of her apartment.

'Why sure was. You know the Doc?' he asked, surprise in his voice, probably at my limey accent.

'You could say I know her, but it was in another life.'

'That's twenty dollars plus tax.'

I handed him a fifty to keep him talking although he needed no encouragement.

'She's a great Doc, fixed my broken arm real good a few months back.' He moved his left arm in several directions to demonstrate. 'As good as new now. Great job.'

'Knows her onions then' I said soon regretting it having to explain but wanting to get after Eve. Now I had found her I did not want to lose her.

Outside looking up and down the street there was no sign of Eve. I had lost her. Had she gone home, or continued her shopping? There were several other shops nearby.

There was nothing for it; I made my way back to her apartment. I began to wonder if this was really such a good idea. Maybe I was trying to catch a tiger by the tail. Should I wait for Peters and the FBI? But I continued purposefully toward 482 Clement Street, not even breaking my stride. No, this was a personal matter between us, a personal score to settle.

Back at the apartment building I did not hesitate in pressing the bell again.

'Hello Rob' said a voice I knew, directly behind me. I had not heard Eve enter the lobby. Silent movement was a good skill, given her other occupation of occasional assassin.

I turned slowly, there she stood, Eve, or Scarlett Maloney, a bag of groceries in her hands a picture of the domestic woman.

It was her; there was no doubt in my mind. The longer black hair could not hide her from me. The blue grey eyes I would never forget, one darker than the other if you looked deeply, if you dared to do so. That was if they allowed you to, today I could, for they were almost lifeless. There was no burning coldness or sparkling life, just a resigned blankness. Her face was blank too, no smile of greeting or frown. She passed by me and opened the lobby door with a key.

'You'd better come in Rob' she called over her shoulder, 'after all you have come a long way.'

The upper floor apartment, one of two, was big and airy. The furniture had a lived in quality, most of it was old, some, perhaps valuable antiques. A large sofa dominated the living room, in front of the obligatory TV. There were several bookcases, with too many books as some were stuffed in random juxtapositions. Quite a few about Ireland, and Pennsylvania, was that where her family had put down roots in the US I wondered? A few pictures were on the walls, landscapes, and one of the Vatican, no pictures or photographs of people.

Eve had gone off into the kitchen with her groceries. The strange thing was I felt safe, in the tiger's lair. If Eve had wanted to kill me she could have done so that night at Gweebarra. And I knew it was her who had sent the postcard, a message of regret.

The big window in the living room looked out toward the Golden Gate Bridge and the coast running north. There were binoculars on a coffee table I picked them up. The coastline beyond the bridge reminded me of Cornwall, with its craggy cliffs all browns and greens.

I recalled reading somewhere that Francis Drake had been one of the first Europeans to find this great bay, when he circumnavigated the globe.

Eve came in from the kitchen with two mugs of coffee and placed them on the table using coasters.

'I think I remember how you liked your coffee Rob, milk one sugar.' She sat on the sofa, tucking her legs under her bottom.

I did not answer; I found this domestic atmosphere unreal and hard to take. I sat on a chair keeping a little distance between us.

'Wary of me Rob?' she smiled for the first time. 'I suppose you have every right to be. How did you manage to find me from that card?'

'Not me Eve, MI5 have been intercepting my mail. Something they do as a matter of course. Apparently the FBI has been watching you as an IRA suspect. Did you go to Ireland a lot? No don't answer, it doesn't really matter now. You were on file at MI5, pictures of you taken at the hospital where you work. They merely put two and two together when the card of Pier 39 arrived they called me in. It was a good bet it was you and now here I am to identify you. But they slipped up, or MI5 did, told me you lived on Clement Street. It was not that difficult to find you Scarlett Maloney, living on Clement Street. And I wanted to see you alone not bursting in on you with the FBI.' I looked down at the floor feeling guilty, but not knowing why.' What do I call you Scarlett or Eve?'

Eve sipped her coffee for a few moments taking the time to think, and waiting for me to look at her which I did. 'I'm Eve for you Rob. I'm sorry; I truly am, for doing away with your Aunt and Bill Longman. But they were going to ruin everything. I'm sure they did not suffer.'

'Doing away' I said laughing loudly 'you murdered them in cold blood Eve, am I supposed to be grateful that, that you put them down painlessly. You are some kind of monster. Would you have done the same to me had I got in your way?'

She shrugged her shoulders 'You don't understand Rob. You're a Brit how could you. You have been raping Ireland without a thought for years.'

'The ends don't justify the means Eve; I'll never understand people like you.'

'And you a professional soldier merely killing for money no matter, rather more important, for us, do you still love me Rob?'

She had me there I did not answer that question; I could not answer it for I did not know. I got up and looked out of the window to hide my face from her. I still could not trust my voice, my emotions were in turmoil. Get a grip I told myself. One thing was certain I had not come all this way merely to serve MI5.

Eve came up behind me and put her arms around me burying her head in my back. Funny I did not flinch. I guessed that answered her question.

'Eve, in time they will come for you. There is nothing for us.'

Eve released me from her embrace, she returned to the sofa. I turned back to her, there were tears on her face. So she was human.

'Rob, what I did was out of conviction, Allan-Cleary was responsible for my Grandfather's execution at the hands of the English, and my Father having to leave Ireland forever destroyed him. I watched him live in exile, something died in him every day. His soul if you like. RP Allan-Cleary had to die at my hand. But it's over now, well almost.'

Eve lapsed into silence; did she expect me to approve what she did? She was no better than many people in the dirty world she inhabited, fanatics; I had come to hate them. But there was something about her.....

'Rob I cannot be taken by the FBI, and then handed over to the Brits to spend years in prison. I could not stand it, I'm a Maloney, that's not for me' she said shaking her head.

'What will you do then Eve, run?'

'I have to think Rob, I have to leave here. I have a cabin a few hours away. I can think there. Will you come with me Rob? Will you help me Rob?'

How could she ask me such a thing? I should refuse, walk right out of that apartment and keep going not looking back but I could not. Instead I said 'Where is the cabin Eve?'

'To the north up in the wine country on Clear Lake, on the eastern shore, pretty isolated and deserted. I think I have kept it secret.'

'They could be watching you now Eve? Even know you have a cabin for all your efforts.'

Eve led me into the bedroom that looked out onto the street. There were cars parked on the street but none had anybody in them as far as we could tell. There were no panel vans either with large aerials, nothing odd out there at all.

We returned to the lounge and I switched on the TV turning the sound up. Then we subjected the apartment to a fine search for bugs but we found nothing. But all a bit late I felt.

After that we communicated with sign language or whispers. Although we had talked normally for several minutes, still we would not give away Eve's plans now. She packed a light weekend bag and we left the apartment in ten minutes. The lobby stairs led down into the basement garage where Eve's car was parked, a yellow Datsun 280ZX sports.

Eve opened the bonnet and boot and we went over the car as finely as we could in five minutes, and found nothing.

'Where you going Scarlet' came a voice I recognised behind us. It was Ian Kagan, bearded now but him alright. We had been too preoccupied searching the car to hear his approach. He held a pistol, looked like a .38, on us midway between us. Obviously he did not trust Eve either.

'Get in the car in the passenger side' he climbed in the back keeping the pistol on Eve. Then she got in behind the wheel.

'Drive' he hissed. He directed her toward the Golden Gate Bridge.

Soon we were passing over the Golden Gate Bridge with the commuter traffic, heading north, darkness was falling. Eve took Interstate 101 north.

Forty-Five

We drove on in silence. A few miles north of the Golden Gate Ian told Eve to turn off onto a minor road; we headed west toward the coast and the sinking sun. Shortly he directed her off onto a track.

'Stop here, everyone out for sightseeing' he giggled, it was an evil sound.

He motioned with the pistol for us to take a path leading toward the cliff edge. There was a sign saying not to go beyond a point we passed, reaching close to the edge we stopped. Down below the Pacific Ocean was crashing against dark jagged rocks. It all reminded me so much of Cornwall. *So this was to be my watery grave* I thought.

'Let him go Ian there's no need for this' said Eve.

'You've gone soft on us Scarlett. We knew when you did not finish him with the injection. No good falling for the enemy. So now I have to execute him. Be a pleasure to finish a Brit Soldier working for the SIS.'

He motioned me to move closer to the edge. But I remained rooted to the spot. What was the point in cooperating, making it easier for him.

Ian took a quick look over the edge. 'Scared of heights' he smirked. 'No matter won't take much to roll you over. You know your people are really arrogant sending you on your own passport. Don't they know we have our own intelligence? And I did try and warn you that night in the pub to leave things be.'

He moved a step closer toward me, bringing the pistol up into a straight arm firing position. My mind was racing. I prepared to rush him. It was a slim chance to put him off his aim.

'Any last...' were the last words he said. Eve flew at him, taking him high up on the shoulder in a clumsy high rugby tackle come barge. They both cartwheeled, arms and legs flailing over the cliff edge. The gun went off harmlessly into the air. I dived to try and grab Eve's legs or an ankle but missed, landing heavily on the ground driving the breath from my lungs.

But I was straight up panting my chest heaving for air. At the edge I looked over. Maybe a hundred or more feet below lay a crumpled body on the jagged dark rocks. The head and neck were at a grotesque angle. But there was only one body and it looked like Ian.

At first I could not see Eve. It took me a few minutes to find her. Thirty of forty feet below she was suspended, held by the stunted trunk and branches of a tree, where no tree had any right to be growing out from the cliff face.

Like most cliffs this one was not sheer, rather it fell steeply down to the sea, interspaced in its length by small plateaus covered by hardy plants.

'Eve' I called. 'Stay still, don't move. I'm on my way.' There was no reply or sign of life. 'Eve' I bellowed. She moved a foot. I could see she was now no longer dazed but clinging on for dear life.

I took off my jacket, removed my belt, putting it in my pocket and started down backwards moving like a crab. Feeling and looking for hand and foot holds, testing my weight on them before trusting them, then moving onto the next one. The light was fading. The wind was fairly strong but at least it was not raining.

How long it took me to get down below Eve I don't know. Then I had to move six feet across the face, the most dangerous movement, to come up with her. Never cross your arms or legs my cliff climbing came back to me, move like a crab.

Eve was sat astride a three inch thick trunk of the tree some sort of pine. Balancing there her feet hanging down either side, while with both hands she held a branch above her head. She was shaking with fear or shock. It was a drop of maybe sixty feet to the rocks below.

'OK Eve, I'm turning around.' With my back to the cliff, I got my feet on a good outcrop of rock on which I could push. With both hands I stretched up clutching Eve's left foot.

'Rob what are you doing.'

'It's OK Eve easy. Look up above the branch you are holding there's another one. See it.'

She nodded.

'I'm going to push you up reach up and grab it stand on the trunk where you are sitting now.'

'I can't it's too far.'

'Yes you can all you need to do is reach, you can do it. If you miss just sit down again but you won't.'

She shook her head.

'Come on Eve do it' I shouted. With that she reached out and I pushed with my legs, and she had the higher branch and was standing on the main trunk closer to its thicker end, a bit safer.

'Moving above you now hang on Eve.'

She nodded her understanding.

I moved back across to the route I had come down and climbed back up. Then moved across the cliff face again to a narrow plateau above the tree. Laying down there wedged against a rock I had little time to regain my breath. I looked down at Eve maybe six feet below. She managed a weak smile at me.

Taking the belt from my pocket I made a loop reversing the belt through the buckle. It was a good strong leather belt; I just hoped the buckle would hold the strain.

'Put one hand through the loop Eve' I said lowering the belt to her. She had to stretch to reach it but managed it while holding on with one hand.

'Now when you're ready grab the belt with your other hand and I'll pull you up. When your legs hit the cliff scramble as hard as you can as if abseiling up the cliff.'

'You'll never hold me Rob, I'll pull you down.'

'Yes I will no fear Eve. Ready!'

Eve nodded.

'After three, one, two, three.' Her weight came on my shoulders with a jolt making them crack. The belt burnt and cut into my hands but I held her pulling up as hard as I could. Then in moments her feet got some purchase, and she was climbing up, her head appeared over the rock in front of me. Her hands were on it holding her weight. Grabbing her under her arms I dragged her up and then got one hand onto the waist band of her jeans and hauled her onto the ledge beside me, where we both collapsed breathing heavily. But we could not rest.

'Come on Eve the light's going. Up you go I'm right behind you're only about twenty feet from the top. Go up like a crab don't cross your legs trying for a hold, you might lose your balance.'

She set off easily the cliff was not that steep on this stretch, and I followed closely.

'Glad I did the Mountain and Artic warfare course. Knew it would come in handy one day' I said.

Eve did not answer concentrating on the task in hand.

Soon we reached the top. Standing there we looked below. It was too dark now to make out Ian's body, maybe the sea had already taken it. All we could see was the white foam of the sea as it crashed against the rocks, and all we could hear was its roar.

'Look at that' said Eve back in the car examining her finger by the car's interior light, 'I've broken two nails.'

With that we both broke into hysterical laughter. Eve began to shake. I took her in my arms and hugged her tight until the shaking stopped.

It was not long after that we left. Eve refused my offer to drive and she soon found her way back onto Interstate 101 heading north.

Forty-Six

At a big filling station Eve filled the tank of the Datsun with petrol, while in the shop I got some toothpaste and a toothbrush, and some shorts as the Americans call underpants. They had a loud flowered pattern on them definitely not me but they would do for a day or two.

At the small town of Santa Rosa, Eve turned off the Interstate onto State Highway 29 heading toward Clear Lake.

We travelled in silence, alone with our thoughts. How long should I give her? Should I encourage her to run? Or give herself up. If I was being patriotic perhaps it should be the latter. But my Aunt had been patriotic, where had it got her? Eve had patriotism of sorts I had to admit, but she had lost that now killing Ian. No that was not even a consideration I realised. It was too difficult. I turned my mind to watching the countryside flash by even though it was dark now. There were signs lit up to camp sites, motels, and vineyards where some proclaimed *'Free Tasting.'*

At the town of Lower Lake we stopped at a diner, neither one of us was hungry. I ate some of the meat loaf I had ordered. Eve just moved her food around the plate I doubted she ate a mouthful. At a late night grocers we got some basic foods, eggs, bread and coffee. In a way it all reminded me of the weekend in Cornwall. But then betrayal had not lain between us.

Eve took the road north along the eastern shore. The lake was black and still, across on its western shore I could see lights winking. Ordinary people there with ordinary concerns, how I wished we could be them. Could we do it or was it just a dream?

About ten miles on Eve slowed, looking for something. "There it is" she said, turning right onto a track which led us another mile through stands of pines. At its end we arrived at a cabin hidden from the road by trees.

It was a fairly small traditional log cabin. Eve unlocked the door and switched on the lights I was surprised it had mains electricity. It had just three rooms, bathroom, open plan kitchen and living room and a large bedroom.

We both showered. Eve had bought two of her bathrobes one for me. I remembered how well one had fitted and felt before.

Eve had lit the large open fire in the lounge by the time I finished my shower. A bottle of whisky stood on a coffee table with glasses.

'Help yourself Rob, it's Irish whisky' she said indicating the bottle, a glass of the amber liquid already in her hand. I poured a large glass and drank deeply, I needed it. Eve was sat in a big armchair, there was another on the opposite side of the fire place where I sat. One of us had put the book I had bought on the coffee table, Eve picked it up.

'*The Great Gatsby,* wonderful book' she leafed through it stroking some of the pages tenderly. 'He dies in the end how ironic' she came across the receipt in the pages, 'you were there today?'

'Yes that's where I first saw you in San Francisco, the owner's quite taken with you. You set his broken arm or something.'

'That's right Rob; you see I have helped some people. Not completely wasted my life, as you might think.'

Eve reached for the bottle and poured a good measure into her glass. 'Drink up Rob, for tomorrow we might die.'

I poured a little more into my glass.

'Being careful Rob, well I figure you have the time' she smiled. Her blue grey eyes were sparkling like they had before, gone was the burning icy glare, was it a trick of the light in them I wondered, or the booze?'

'They say F.Scott Fitzgerald died of the booze quite young too, the trumpeter of the Jazz Age, that's what they call him.'

'Irish I suppose?' I asked.

'His mother was of Irish extraction, like me' Eve giggled, 'his father a southern gentleman. Don't know if he was Irish with a name like Fitzgerald, you would think so. Might, I say might' she slurred her words slightly 'have been Scottish not that it really matters. His parents mixed up old Scott for sure. Gave him a guilt complex, sent him to a Catholic boarding school you see. That's what they did to me. We are a real mixed up people. It was my mother's idea to call me Scarlett, after O'Hara in the film. Her favourite film *Gone With the Wind.* Mum had Irish roots too. You see my history has dictated what I would be as much as any genes might.' Then she fell silent gazing into the fire at some far away memory.

I could not agree with Eve's theory of the past dictating what a person should be but said nothing, what did I know. 'How did you get away from Gweebarra, Eve?'

'Oh that was easy Rob. I went back the way we had come picked up my bag followed the hedgerow down to the road then walked over to Mount Edgcumbe, well ran most of the way you had shown me. From Cremyll a passenger ferry to Plymouth. A taxi to the bus station a bus to Wales. From Swansea the ferry to Cork I had my US passport. Within forty-eight hours I was back home here in California. The only thing I regretted was what I did to you Rob. I sincerely hope with all my heart you believe me?'

I did not answer Eve I had nothing to say.

Finally Eve got to her feet; she was quite steady even though she had drunk over half the bottle. 'Forgot the sheets for the bed Rob we will have to make do with blankets, I have some here' she disappeared into the bedroom, I heard her moving about.

'It's made to a fashion Rob' she said returning and filling her glass again. There was only an inch or so left in the bottle now.

'Yes, old F.Scott was right with Gatsby. Come on Rob drink up you're dropping behind. That's the trouble with you English cannot hold your liquor. We Irish get friendly, the English violent. Look at your football supporters always fighting after a few beers.'

Eve sat in silence then, briefly she studied me, I found I could hold her stare, and it was she who looked away this time with a sigh.

I drank no more, wanting to keep a clear head, and my wits about me. Why had I agreed to this, what was going to happen, could I trust Eve? Yet she had saved my life twice, at Gweebarra she had disobeyed orders, and by killing Ian. And I had saved her from the cliff. The bond between us was strong.

Eve drained her glass in three gulps wiping her mouth with the back of her hand. She looked at the bottle. 'No more for me Rob, I think you might be right. Are you coming to bed Rob? I would appreciate someone close tonight.'

We lay on soft blankets covered by a blanket. At first separated by a few inches but finally in each other's arms. I think Eve was awake all night. She said nothing and moved little but she was awake. I dozed fitfully.

With the coming of dawn Eve woke me with a kiss, there was a little greyness outside. We had not pulled the curtains. It was perhaps 4am when we made love. I was powerless to resist her. I knew then I could not deign Eve anything. After I slept again easily, nothing really mattered then.

Forty-Seven

Eve woke me, it was still early but fully light. She sat on the bed dressed in a thin white dress, no more than a night dress that came down to her knees.

'I want you to do something for me Rob, will you get dressed please?'

Eve was calm yet determined; the drink from the night before seemed to have had no effect on her. Quickly I washed my face not shaving, I felt fuzzy headed from lack of sleep and the whisky had not helped. She waited patiently while I got ready. It was only five minutes and I was ready, she still only wore the dress I knew she had nothing else on underneath it.

Eve led me outside, she carried a large handbag. It was still cold, the grass covered in frozen dew, I thought about 6am, perhaps it was earlier, but I had forgotten to put my watch on. She said nothing but walked toward the trees. There she led us onto a path, it passed through the pines and redwoods and Douglas spruce. We walked in silence. The trees smelt heavily of fresh pine, nothing moved, not a sound from bird or insect as if leaving us alone. Did they know what lay ahead?

Presently we arrived at a small beach of sandy shingle on the lake shore; it was inside a partly hidden horseshoe bay, you would have to know it was there to find it from the lake or shore. Out beyond it the lake looked big, as indeed it was the biggest in the State. Big and black, the water still, as if brooding. The sky was ice blue, when the sun got higher the surface of the lake would change. I felt cold.

'Eve you must be freezing in that thin dress, why have we come here?'

She turned toward me putting down her bag, she ignored my question.

'This lake is over two million years old created by primeval volcanic forces. It's deep Rob, oh so deep.'

Eve turned toward the lake looking out over the black waters she shuddered slightly. 'So much older than us, it will be here long after we are gone.'

She kicked off her shoes her toes clutching slightly at the sandy grey shingle, and then she knelt opening her bag, from which she took a Browning Automatic pistol, gun metal grey with a black butt. A powerful weapon, I had fired one before a long time ago.

My intake of breath was sharp, as if it wasn't me, somehow divorced from me, surely not after all this I thought. After all we had been through. But I said nothing.

Eve stood and ejected the magazine from the butt of the pistol. I could see the brass jackets of the bullets with their deadly lead heads in the magazine. She replaced the magazine with a metallic click, released the safety catch and cocked the weapon with the top slide bringing a round into the chamber, it was ready to fire. Then holding it by the barrel she held it out to me butt first.

Taking the weapon I did not question her just held it cold in my hand pointing at the ground and waited. What on earth did she want?

Eve turned and stared out over the lake, the minutes ticked by and we stood there without moving. Me looking at her, Eve looking at the lake, time meant nothing. A slight breeze had started from the south lightly rippling the surface of the lake, and making the lakeside trees whisper, and moving the bottom of Eve's dress.

'Rob' said Eve without turning, 'I cannot run, that's not for me, looking over my shoulder all the time no. The Brotherhood will come looking for me now when Ian makes no report, even if his body is not washed up somewhere. They will come looking. They will not rest. You heard what he said; I was marked as untrustworthy letting you live.

And somehow they knew you had come here looking for me. They never give up Rob see how long they waited to execute Allan-Cleary. No I cannot run.

And I cannot rot in a British, or come to that, American prison. There is nothing for me now but death.' She hurried on, hardly stopping for breath; as if now she had started she could not stop, and perhaps in an attempt to stop me arguing.

'Death comes to all of us, in a way it's a privilege to choose when. I wish I could shoot myself but I cannot. Funny that' she giggled but there was no hysteria in it 'when I have shot others. But I cannot do it not to myself, though I can drown myself. So Rob, shortly I'm going to walk into the lake and drown myself, but that's slow and hard and takes willpower, I might not manage it the first time, we all have a natural will to live, but I will do it. The cold water will help. This lake is oh so cold, cold fresh water from the mountain snows. Will you shoot me Rob when I walk out there? Do you love me enough to do that; will you help me in this final act?'

Eve turned back to me and moved closer to me. The blue grey eyes examined mine. Funny I felt her voice had acquired a slight Irish accent.

'I don't want to Eve, but you know I will do anything for you. Yes I will do it.' Was it me talking, I wondered how calm I was; perhaps I knew she was right.

'When it's done Rob.'

I turned away from her shaking my head. Gently she took my arms bringing me back to face her. Waiting until my eyes met hers.

'When it is done Rob take my bag and dress back to the car. Empty the cabin, I have packed up everything you need to take, remember your book. Take the car, park it near the Golden Gate Bridge.

Hopefully when they find it you will be long gone, they will think I have jumped from the bridge. It's not likely they will find my body here. With no tides the lake will be my grave forever. Remember your book.' Her voice was flat without emotion.

'Surely Eve there is another way. I'll come with you we can find somewhere. South America lots of people disappear there, start a new life.

"No Rob" she shook her head, her hair swinging in a curtain around her face.

"No you would come to resent me; I might you. What would we be Butch Cassidy and the Sundance Kid, or Bonnie and Clyde. No it's over for me Rob, for us but not you. Listen to me Rob do as I say with the car. Please Rob.'

I nodded, I could not speak. Even now, even after death she had to be in control. Eve took my left hand, in the right was the gun, and squeezed it.

'Try to hit me at the base of the neck Rob high up on my back should sever the spine. But anywhere high up on my torso will be quick. Not the arms or anything Rob a good shot, I trust you. I trust you more than anyone else.'

Eve removed her white dress over her head. The nipples of her bare breasts stood pink and erect from the cold. From around her neck she took off a crucifix and chain and from a finger a signet ring, she handed them to me.

'Keepsakes for you Rob. Don't think too badly of me Rob. Live for both of us' and she leaned forward and kissed me briefly and lightly on the lips. I could say nothing there was a great lump in my throat.

Eve turned away from me toward the lake. She sighed lightly and began walking slowly in three steps she reached the water. She did not hesitate but kept going with the same steady step. She did not look back.

The lake shelved steeply. At twenty feet the water was up to the bottom of her breasts. The wind had dropped again nothing moved on the surface of the lake. Just a slight ripple coming back to the shore from Eve, as she walked on into the black water.

I raised the pistol sighting as I had been taught. Right hand around the pistol grip finger on the trigger, left hand under the butt so you held the gun steady on a platform of your left hand, it all came back to me, and with a short barrelled weapon it was easy to miss. Forget all those films. It is difficult to hit a barn door at any range but point blank with a pistol. And I was not that good a shot never had been.

I concentrated hard, it had to be right, and I sighted on her upper back below the neck. I took up the trigger pressure, squeeze don't pull. The guns bang was loud almost deafening after the silence.

The bullet took Eve exactly where she had wanted it as if she had willed it to that spot, and I was merely her tool, her compliant executioner. The power flung her forward into the water. She was gone into the consuming blackness of the lake. By some freak her right arm pointed momentarily to the sky and then slid away following her body into the depths and she was gone.

Dropping my arm still holding the gun I sobbed loudly only once, and then flung the pistol with all my might far out into the lake.

Reaching down I picked up her dress which lay crumpled where she had left it, pressing it to my face I breathed deeply, to smell her before it faded and was gone forever. How long I stood there with the dress I do not know.

At last I picked up her shoes and bag and made my way along the path back to the cabin. There I did as Eve had instructed, packed up the car and checked the cabin carefully. I did not go back to the lake side again. After locking the cabin I sat in the car for a few minutes.

There was no point lingering, what for I told myself, it had not been a dream it might seem dreamlike but it had all happened. Even if I wished it had been a dream. Starting the car I took the track back to the main road.

Epilogue.

It was mid morning by the time I parked the Datsun in the Golden Gate Bridge car park, on the San Francisco side of the bridge. There for tourists to park their hire cars and who might want to walk out onto the bridge for a closer look at the great landmark. It was a grey overcast day threatening rain. All I took from the car was the cross chain and ring and the book, everything else I left in the car, including the keys with any luck some thief might steal it. And then the car would not be found and no trace of Eve at all.

Taking a bus back into the city I got off at Cathedral Hill and walked the sort distance to my hotel. At reception there were no messages for me. That surprised me for it seemed like a life time had passed over the last few hours. But that was all it had been, less than twenty-four hours. It felt like a lifetime to me.

I began to wonder why Eve had fought so hard to live on the cliff. Why had she not jumped then, flung herself to her death on the rocks, it would have been quick. Perhaps she had preferred her watery grave. Perhaps it was merely a fear of heights. Did she plan it all no I could not believe that? I was glad we had that last night together, it would have to last a lifetime for me.

Despair gripped me like a vice and I spent most of my time in my hotel room. Trying to analyse why I felt so bad at the death of a terrorist murderer who had killed my own aunt, while I drank my way through the contents of the mini bar, and when that was gone, room service brought up more booze and some food of which I ate little.

'Hello Rob' said Andy Peters when he rang on the third day of the binge I was on. "It looks like our bird has flown".

'What' I said loudly through my drunken haze.

'That is Rob Nicolson?' said Peters.

'Yes hello Andy I'm fine' I said concentrating trying not to slur my words, 'what were you saying?'

'Yes I'm afraid the FBI has lost her. It's all been rather a waste of time. You can stay on if you like; I could swing a day or two more?'

'No that's alright Andy, good of you but I'd like to get back.'

'OK Rob I'll book you on tonight's flight to London. Do you want me to see you off?'

'No thanks Andy I'll manage.'

I stopped the booze there and then. The answer to my black dog did not lie in the bottom of a glass. There was no answer as such. I had to lock it away, or it would drive me mad, take it out when I was stronger.

The next morning I was back in London, none of my loving family had missed me either. No reason why they should have. It just felt to me so hard with nobody I could even tell or ever tell. It would be my secret for eternity.

Dawn had missed me and I could not lift my morose mood even for her, or tell her anything. She soon dumped me; just as well really, she deserved better, a good girl.

Major Lanyon phoned me at work apologising for the, 'FBI cock-up.' Thanked me for my efforts, and finished with a 'Stay in touch old man.' He seemed in a hurry probably wanting to get at his rock cakes. 'Stay in touch' that was a laugh and something I would not be doing I had had enough of his dark murky world. He would have to learn himself that somehow the IRA had known of my movements. Perhaps there was a mole in the FBI.

Eve did not leave me right away. I put her cross and chain and ring away in the bottom of a drawer. During the day I could focus on other things. But at night, in my dreams, she came back to me. Sometimes just as a beautiful naked woman walking into the water of a black lake, often she did look back at me and smile. Sometimes I woke crying her name.

But in time even this receded. I stopped trying to analyse myself and just locked it away like the cross and chain and ring.

Six months later, in the spring of 1985 I took a holiday to Northern Cyprus. Mother still bizarrely had some of Aunt Carolyn's ashes I took some with me, scattering part beside my Grandfather's grave in the weedy, overgrown Kyrenia Protestant Cemetery.

In a hire car I visited Kantara lying at the extreme eastern end of the saw tooth Kyrenia Mountains, toward the Karpas peninsula.

There, a mile or so from the Crusader Castle after which the village of Kantara was named I found my legacy, my bungalow, all boarded up. I wondered who had taken the trouble to do that. It was shaded from the sun like the other dozen or so abandoned bungalows shaded by pines and cypress trees. Prising open one of the doors I managed to squeeze inside. All was dry. There was no real sign of my Grandfather's and Aunt's occupation, just the odd piece of furniture that must have been theirs, now blistered and dry.

Outside I walked right around the bungalow and through the overgrown garden, in which was a dried up fountain. I tried to imagine how it once was. On the front wall in faded red paint Eoka-B graffiti from 1974 proclaimed *'Enosis or death.'* I smiled at that should it have read *'Enosis or the Turks'* I thought. I scattered the rest of Aunt Carolyn's ashes there. They were taken up by the dry breeze blowing from Africa and whisked away into the air. Somehow I thought they might mingle with her dear Joe who had died in Africa. The trip to Cyprus did much to restore me.

Back in my flat a few weeks later looking for a book to read I picked up *'The Great Gatsby'* and opened it. For the first time I noticed Eve had written inside the front cover on the blank page. *'Thank you Rob. Live for both of us. Love Eve xxx.'*

Authors Note

Most of the characters in *Room 39 and the Cornish Legacy* are entirely fiction and any resemblance to real persons, living or dead is purely coincidental. Actual historical characters are genuine, even if their actions and locations deviate from reality in places.

Of course Ian Fleming and Admiral John Godfrey did work for Naval Intelligence in Rooms 38 and 39 at the Admiralty. Also Edward Merett was Admiral Godfrey's personal secretary. The Ultra decodes of the German Enigma Machines arrived in Room 13, known as *'Lenin's tomb'*. Commander Frank Slocum was in charge of SIS operations in Cornwall during World War II. An aircraft was lost to a mysterious explosion, which may have been sabotage, flying with gold and agents for Algeria albeit in 1944, and was observed by the Home Guard crashing into the sea off Watergate Bay.

The Ankara cell of German Agents did exist in the Levant during World War II.

While the raid to capture or kill Rommel was taking place 'Operation Flipper'. A high priority signal was decrypted at the secret office of British Intelligence at GHQ Cairo. The signal was from MI6 in London. Bletchley Park had just decoded a message from German Army Enigma which revealed that Lieutenant General Erwin Rommel was on his way back to Libya and would arrive the following day, 18 November. He had spent the past three weeks in Rome, spending part of the time with his wife Lucie. For the sake of my story I have moved this message forward in time by a few days.

The Abwehr the German counter-espionage service did use book titles for code names hence White Fang from the Jack London book.

Acknowledgments

Particular thanks go to my wife Margaret as always for her editing and proof reading skills, the more so with this book as it was her idea to set it in Cornwall. Kelvyn and Catherine Maunder, good friends of mine, were extremely helpful with their reflections on the Downderry area of Cornwall where they lived during the time period of this book the 1980's. John Sherress for reading the manuscript and his good ideas on the same.

The following books have been useful.
Get Rommel. Michael Asher. Weidenfeld & Nicolson 2004.
Secret Service. Christopher Andrew. Heinemann 1985.
Operation Cicero. L.C.Moyzisch. Readers Union 1952.
Cornwall at war 1939-1945. Peter Hancock. Halsgrove 2002.
The Life of Ian Fleming. John Pearson. Jonathan Cape 1966.
Room 39 Naval Intelligence in action 1939-45 Donald McLachlan. Weidenfeld & Nicolson 1968.
Military Intelligence in Cyprus. Panagiotis Dimitrakis. I.B.Tauris 2010.
A Secret history of the IRA. Ed Moloney. Allan Lane 2002.
A Pictorial view of Downderry and Seaton. Kevin Reilly & Jo Lanyon. Lithiack Press 1985.
March to the South Atlantic. 42 Commando Royal Marines in the Falklands War. Nick Vaux. Buchan & Enright Publishers 1986.
No Picnic Julian Thompson. Cassell & Co 1985.
The Game of the Foxes. Ladislas Farago. David McKay Company. 1971.
And finally of course to *The Great Gatsby and F.Scott Fitzgerald. April 10 1925 Charles Scribner's & Sons.*

Liskeard, Cornwall 2012.

ENDS